THE LIGHTHOUSE KEEPER'S SON

THE LIGHTHOUSE KEEPER'S SON

Dallas Edward Quidley Jr.

PUBLISHING

an imprint of The Reader's Digest Association, Inc.

LifeRich Publishing books may be ordered
through booksellers or by contacting:

LifeRich Publishing
1663 Liberty Drive
Bloomington, IN 47403
www.liferichpublishing.com
1 (888) 238-8637

Because of the dynamic nature of the Internet, any web addresses or
links contained in this book may have changed since publication and
may no longer be valid. The views expressed in this work are solely those
of the author and do not necessarily reflect the views of the publisher,
and the publisher hereby disclaims any responsibility for them.

"Drum Point Lighthouse" Used With Permission From Mary Lou Troutman
"B 29" Used with Permision from Stephan C Brown. Commemorative Air Force.
"Cape Hatteras Lighthouse" Used with Permission from Drew Wilson. Virginia Pilot

Any people depicted in stock imagery provided by Thinkstock are
models, and such images are being used for illustrative purposes only.
Certain stock imagery © Thinkstock.

ISBN: 978-1-4897-0079-7 (sc)
ISBN: 978-1-4897-0080-3 (e)

Library of Congress Control Number: 2013919704

Printed in the United States of America.

LifeRich Publishing rev. date: 01/10/14

INTRODUCTION

S TUDYING OVER 500 YEARS OF his ancestor's lives has influenced the writer of this book to do a memoir of his life for his descendants. He hopes that many others will enjoy his lighthouse family, his Air Force travels and all his experiences. He believes that Christianity and Common Sense have been his "rod and staff" thereby bringing him comfort and joy. He wishes to share his life with you.

This book is a History, a Genealogy and a series of many Short Stories. It is intended to remind you that a successful and good life must be a busy and hard working life to achieve a modicum of happiness with above average prosperity. A great life is yours to make. Remember that all good and bad things begin with you.

These stories are real but a few might have been slightly enhanced due to the thankful memories of the writer. With fading memory he knows that the Holy Spirit must have been guiding his hands and his thoughts as he wrote.

Since this book is a chronology structured book of short stories you will encounter a few duplications of people and places. This ensures that every story has full content. You will enjoy the intermingling of people and places. As you travel thru time in the book you will get to know the characters better; hope you will enjoy their friendship and love. Life can be confusing but in time everything comes to a good and happy ending. Hope you get that feeling about this literary adventure. Enjoy.

The Ancestry Content was written to make you more aware of your ancestors, and to encourage you to seek information about every aspect of your heritage. This part might bore you until you determine that ancestry does play a role in the transformation of your body, mind and sometimes your soul.

If you don't laugh a little and shed a few tears while reading these stories, you might not be as normal as you think. This book could be the personality test you have been seeking

Maybe you should write your own book. You know your family better than anyone else. You may use this format to start putting your data together. Start your research now. Why not visit your local library? You might find that you are already on a family tree. Another place to start is at your local History Society; visit one of their meetings and tell the group about your family tree.

If you still have a grandma or aunt, ask for their advice in searching your ancestors. The Family Bible might have a Family Tree in it. Look for information on the internet; It is full of data and some of it is free.

If needed there are professional genealogist who can trace your family for you as far back as possible.

Good luck and may God Bless you.

Dallas

This compilation of people, events, time and places follow

ANCESTRY OF SADIE RAE PITTMAN (QUIDLEY)
(Wife of The Lighthouse Keeper's Son)

Capt Thomas Pittman	1610 Eng
	1651 VA
& Widow of William Gwaltney	Begat
Obedience Pittman	1650 Eng
	1712 VA
& Unk	Begat
Joseph Pittman	1680 VA
	1752 Adams Creek NC
& Elizabeth Ferguson	1748-1809 Begat
Thomas Pittman	1715-179
& Unk	Begat
Joseph Pittman	1746-1832
& Mary Neal	Begat
John Pittman	1785-1852
& Abigail Smith	1792-1855 Begat

Meredith Pittman   1821-1894
& Mary Elizabeth Lewis   1829-1897 Begat

Henry Pittman   1853-1934
& Margaret E Banks   1845-1902 Begat

James Winfield Pittman   16 Jul 1880
                            30 Apr 1972
& Missouri C Tosto   1882-1962 Begat

Robert Pittman Sr   11 Aug 1901
                            31 Oct 1961
& Eva Mae Banks   14 Nov 1909
                            27 Jun 1991 Begat

Sadie Rae Pittman   31 Dec 1929
& Dallas E Quidley Jr   26 Jan 1929

ANCESTRY OF DALLAS EDWARD QUIDLEY JR

(The Lighthouse Keeper's Son)

Capt John Quidley	1640 Devonshire Eng Nansemond Co VA
& Unknown	Begat
Thomason Quidley	1662 Nansemond Co VA
& Unknown	Begat
Patrick Quidley	1681 VA NC
& Unknown	Begat
Capt William Quidley	1720 NC Buxton NC
& Sarah Jane	1722 NC Begat
John Quidley	1749 Buxton NC Buxton NC
& Asah	1752 NC Buxton NC Begat
William Quidley	1775 Buxton NC 1830 Buxton NC
& Nancy Rollison	1776 Buxton NC 1820 Buxton NC Begat

William Quidley Jr	1807 Buxton NC
	1859 Englehard NC
& Elizabeth Farrow	1809 Buxton NC
	1859 Englehard NC Begat
LHK David F Quidley	1847 Buxton NC 1902
	Buxton NC
& Rovenia Rollison	1864 Buxton NC
	1955 Buxton NC Begat
LHK Thomas D Quidley	1882 Buxton NC
	1980 New Bern NC
& Lorena Mae Rawls	1890 Stonewall NC
	1936 Hobucken NC Begat
LHK Dallas E Quidley Sr	1908 Pamlico NC
	1990 New Bern NC
& Lena Mae Swindell	1909 Merritt NC
	1997 New Bern NC Begat
M Sgt Dallas E Quidley Jr	1929 PamlicoNC
& Sadie Rae Pittman	1929 Lukens NC Begat
Dallas E Quidley III	1952 Cherry PT MCAS NC
Harold A Quidley	1954 Lake Charles AFB LA

THE LIGHTHOUSE KEEPER'S SON

2 Dec 1847

David Farrow Quidley born 0n Hatteras Island NC (died 1 Aug 1902) (Wife Rovenia Simpson Rollison-born 16 May 1864 9 died 3 Sep 1955) He was a Surfman on the beach at Kinnekeet NC riding a horse watching for sailing ships that had

hit the beach or grounded off shore. As a surfman it was his job to signal the Station to send additional help and the equipment to save the ship and/or crew. Later in his life he was a Lighthouse Keeper and also he was the first person to transport mail by boat daily from Englehard NC to Hatteras Island

Dallas Edward Quidley Jr.

15 JUL 1882

Thomas Daniels Quidley born on Hatteras Island NC (died 12 Aug 1980) (Wife Lorena Mae Rawls born 4 May 1890 (Died 6 Jan 1936)

He began his Lighthouse Keeping career at 16 when he had a six month temporary job of fueling the lamp, lighting it and turning it off, and keeping the many steps of Cape Hatteras Lighthouse clean. He also served at Bodie Island LH, Neuse River LH and Hobucken USLHS Life Saving Station and Buoy Yard.

11 Aug 1901

Robert Pittman Sr born in Lukens NC Carteret County (died 31 Oct 1961) (Wife:Eva Mae Banks born 14 Nov 1908 (Died 27 Jan 1990

Robert was a fisherman, shrimper, crabber and oysterman. He owned his own boats (the last one was the EVA, a forty foot Cannon Built trawler). In his off season of his water work, Robert was an excellent carpenter and builder. From 1922 to 1924 Robert served in the US Geodetic Service surveying and making maps in the USA and Africa.

2 Dec 1908

Dallas Edward Quidley Sr born in Pamlico NC Pamlico County (Died 14 Feb 1991) (Wife: Lena Mae Swindell-born 22 Apr 1909 (Died 4 Feb 1997) Dallas Sr became a part of the US Lighthouse Service when he did two part time jobs when he was 17 and 18. He was selected to fill in as a crew member on the US Lightship Diamond Shoals to give vacation relief to the regular crew. At 20 he joined the USCG but was injured and he went back home after hospitalization. Then in the 1930s he was an Assistant LHK at Neuse River Entrance LH and several other lighthouse service facilities. In 1937 he became LH Keeper to keep the light and safety devices going , and prepare the lighthouses for eventual closing, In that capacity he was LHK at Cristfield MD, Solomons MD and Ronoake Island NC. He took lighthouse keeping and his Coast Guard duty seriously.

1 Aug 1925

Dallas Quidley Sr, as a young man in his last two years of high school was employed as a vacation fill-in so that the regular crew of the Diamond Shoals Lightship could have a two week vacation. This was a temporary position for Dallas Sr and was obtained through the recommendation of the area US Congressman. In those years the Congressmen and Senators selected qualified people from their districts to fill US jobs. Due to his marine engine knowledge and marine life, Dallas Sr got the same job for a short period in 1925. He was 17 in 1925 and 18 in 1926. A letter of commendation for both years of service is in the Dallas Quidley Sr files.

Jan 1927

Dallas Quidley Sr joined the US Coast Guard and was immediately stationed on Long Island NY. He began his dream Coast Guard career. To start he was a basic seaman and after that he became an Engine Specialist and 2nd Mate. The 1st Mate was the Capt of the boat and the 2nd Mate usually ran and maintained the engines. The entire crew of a Patrol boat this size did not need over four people to operate it.

Dec 1928

DEQ Sr was severely injured in a fire and explosion on the Coast Guard Patrol boat on Long Island NY. His partner on duty with him in the engine room was killed. Dallas was hospitalized for several months and then released from the hospital. On his signed request and promise not to hold the USCG responsible, he was honorably discharged from the USCG on 16 March 1929.

After fully recuperating at home in Pamlico NC, Thomas Daniels Quidley, his dad, put him in charge of the sports fishing boat, The Tutt. The twenty one year old, already an experienced seaman, Capt Dallas Sr took customers on fishing trips in Pamlico Sound and into the Atlantic Ocean. The Tutt operated from the Quidley Dock in the village of Pamlico on lower Broad Creek.

Due to the financial depression of the country and lack of local industry, except "bootlegging" (illegal alcohol manufacturing and selling), Dallas Sr was thankful that his dad, Thomas D Quidley, began several startup businesses to give Dallas Sr a chance.

Capt Tom added another business which was pulling boats out of the water for painting and repairs. This was accomplished by floating the boat on a wheeled carriage, then pulling the boat and carriage out of the water on a rail drawn by a horse or by the recently invented gasoline engine.

Those two small enterprises fed the Dallas Quidley Sr family (and several other village men employed by Dallas or Tom Quidley). In those days it took above average intelligence and a lot of hard work to make a good living for each family, but LHK T D Quidley devised several business structures to keep his family, neighbors and friends, all working and functioning in the hard times of the1920s and early 30s.

Sometimes all the above jobs were not sufficient to keep the family going Dallas therefore also outfitted with the aid of his father, a smaller boat for crabbing in the local creeks. There was a new process for catching blue crabs. The new process took only one person for the job. A beef or a pork strip was tied to the crab line about two feet apart for the entire length of the line, normally one hundred feet long. The small boat was rowed with a set of oars, and the boat was equipped with a protruding side boom holding a special guide to keep the line straight as it traveled over the boom as the operator rowed his boat forward. Crabs would turn loose of the bait and fall into the scoop or small net just before going over the boom. It was like the crabs were jumping into the boat. If there were any crabs to catch that day or in that place the work was fun even if it was hard work.

Your catch of crabs could be a full wooden farm barrel or no crabs at all. Your luck and not your hard work made you a successful crabber. Often someone else would beat you to your best location. If the water was choppy due to wind or rain that might keep the crabs from grabbing the bait and holding onto the line long enough to come out of the water and drop into the scoop or net.

Dallas Sr did an excellent job of trying to provide for his family. He worked hard but his aspirations deluded him by is not being able to pay on time for 40 unused farm barrels. This proved the first big disappointment of his early life. Let us see how that happened:

The 20 year old disabled veteran of the Coast Guard came home to a new life to enjoy his new baby son and build a bigger family. He had dreams of being a member of the Masons and eventually, like his father and his uncles, become a Shriner. That was the social thing to do and he wanted to be a good citizen helping his fellow man.

As soon as any young man can afford the fees and get the time to study the rules and the ritual of the mystic organization, he can make application to join the Masonic Order When the application is approved he then has to go before the entire membership of the local Lodge; the members vote by using a white and black ball as ballots. One black ball is all it takes to stop you from becoming a member. The member who votes is supposed to be an outstanding citizen with a solid reputation for being a good neighbor, and also being an intelligent human being.

In due time Dallas was ready to begin his journey into the mystery of the local historical order of the

Masons. His application went to the membership for the ball voting. Dallas Sr's father and his father in law were at the meeting where the voting was in progress. One black ball was cast for Dallas Sr. He was quietly devastated and disturbed, but as a gentleman with respect for the Masonic Order, he never mentioned the Masons or his black ball again; Not even to his family but surely he must have discussed it with his wife Lena. She too never mentioned it to anyone.

His personality changed because of this black balled experience. It was obvious to his family that he would never again be interested in competing for any goal. When his son Dallas Jr was a Mason himself, his grandfather Will Swindell confessed he saw the black ball drop into the voting box. Grandfather Will, whom Dallas called "Granna Will", in order that Dallas Jr would forever understand his dad's erratic behavior of the past, confessed this information that helped Dallas Jr understand his dad of many years.. The overdue revelation and confession helped to sooth Granna Will's own conscious. Will Swindell had always been super faithful to the Lodge. He was a very honest man and kept his oath to the Masonic Order not to divulge anything that went on at meeting with outsiders. Dallas Jr was no longer an outsider, but in a few months he demitted from the organization for other reasons. Respect for his grandfather grew. His love and understanding of his own dad sky rocketed.

Granna Will told Dallas Jr that it was the husband of one of Will's sisters that did the dirty work. Granna Will also told Dallas Jr about other mean and sinister things his brother in law had done that he also knew about.

Mr Will said he knew that Dallas Sr had tried to return the unused barrels but they were refused. The black-ball affect never left Dallas Sr's mind. It had been the worst disaster of his adult life since the USCG boat fire and explosion. The black ball was like a curse that was put on Dallas Sr for the remainder of his life. He was never the same person after he was 21 years old. He and his immediate family could have seen much more happiness had it not been for the damned black ball.

Jan 1929

Dallas Edward Quidley Jr born in Pamlico NC and delivered by Dr James Purdy in the front left bedroom of the Thomas D Quidley home. Ms Georgianna Willis assisted the Dr in the birthing process, and she also became his Nanny and friend for her lifetime. Georgianna died in 1948. Dallas will never forget his visits to her home with the newspaper wallpaper and the delicious molasses cake. Georgianna worked for a dollar a day. Dallas Jr has a cancelled bank bank check to her to prove that.

DEC 1929

Sadie Rae Pittman Born in Lukens NC, Carteret County, in her parent's home on the high banks of South River with her great grandmother, Sarah Pittman Edwards the mid wife and nurse in Sadie's delivery. Sadie lived in her parent's home until it was moved from Lukens to Oriental in 1943.Their house moving trips in 1943 were all made on her dad's boat. The home in pieces was floated five miles across the Neuse River. Sadie had helped her dad take the home completely apart and label every board, window, door etc. for the move and the reassembly. On both sides of the river, the move was tedious, ardent and very time consuming. It was a job.

The move from Lukens Island to Oriental was a big decision in which all the family participated. The decision came fairly easy after Sadie, the oldest child, had to live away from home during her first year of High School. Her first through seventh school years was in a one room school house on the island taught by good teachers from the mainland. The parents helped the good teachers. Her grandfather, Storekeeper Henry Banks, was in charge of teacher selection. The final school year at Lukens Sadie was the teacher's assistant. For a young girl of fourteen that was great management experience and special training. The learning experiences gave her insight for the future and even from the one-room school she was ready for a four year high school with better facilities and plenty of teachers. She started ninth grade at Oriental High School and graduated from there in May 1948.

Her last teacher at Lukens School was Ms Grace Wilson who had such great confidence in Sadie she thought Sadie would pursue a teaching degree and become a dedicated teacher like herself.

Sadie Rae Pittman, her brothers Bob and Tom and her sister Dot all graduated from high school. Bob then joined the U S Coast Guard, finished his military service and graduated from NCSU with a degree in marine biology. Tom graduated from the new Pamlico County High School at Bayboro NC, then went in the US Army then graduated from East Carolina University with a degree in business and finance. Sadie's oldest brother James Henry retired from the USCG. Sadie's two sons have college degrees and have been very successful in their fields. Sadie's five daughters in law all have college degrees and two of them have higher degrees.

All are retired except Susan Rogers who is Vice President of NRG, one of the most important energy corporations in America. On 17 Jan 2013 she was honored by the NY Stock Exchange to ring the opening bell for the day. That was a super honor for Susan and her husband, Dallas Edward Quidley III and both their families. Susan and Ed also had retired from Progress Energy in NC. Ed continued to work in nuclear energy as a Plant Manager. He is now engaged in consultation and training at several nuclear plants for short periods of work as a contractor. Ed invented an electronic part that revolutionized the sound for the amplifier industry. Previously guitar amps had a limited capacity to control the volume of the sound. Ed's new invention was put into a new amplifier that he developed. His amps are called "Quidley Amps" and are being sold without much advertising.

Sadie's five daughters in law honor Sadie with great love and admiration for being a continuing housewife, mother, grandmother and mother in law. One daughter in law, Karen Edmonds Quidley, went through chemo treatments, two months hospitalization, and breast surgery and is permanently on oxygen. She had breast cancer and survived. Sadie's visitations and her prayers for Karen are unending. Sadie says Karen was the best working mother she has ever seen. Karen also might believe that Sadie is the best non-working mother she has ever seen. Karen has a degree in computer science and she is a part of several break-thru inventions that made home and vehicle use of the computer a giant boost in education and business. Prior to her cancer she was a leading computer program designer; her success has been comparable to the growth in computer use worldwide.

17 Oct 1933

Willoughby Thomas Quidley, Billy, was born in Pamlico NC in the home of his grandfather Thomas D Quidley. Dr James Purdy delivered Billy. He was destined to be the hardest working, most personable, kindest and most generous of all Dallas and Lena Quidley's children. His work with Harvey Brothers Service Station at the foot of the Neuse River Bridge in Bridgeton NC brought many additional customers and friends to stop by where Billy was the star attraction. He gave better automobile service than anyone before or after him. at that location; he went from there to the New Bern Fire Department where he carried on the same helpful attitude in the fire and rescue line as well as help to anyone who visited the firehouse when he was on duty. He married Verna Rose Bland from Oriental. They had one child Vicky Lynn Quidley. Vicky married Larry Nobles and they had Mark and Chad. Then she married Jerry Gladson and they had Cody Gladson. Billy was proud of his family and always gave his grandsons lots of helpful attention.

For many years Billy held three jobs; City Fireman, Seashore Bus Co driver a Chemical truck driver. In his spare time he helped anyone he saw in need such as to rebuild an engine for an old lady who did not have money for a new car or repairs, and so many more He mainly gave his time and talents to anyone he saw in need of them. For all his work, he probably got more back than he or anyone else actually realized. After all, God did keep Billy helping others. Even on his death bed he was telling one grandson how to tear down an automobile transmission and put it together again. He never stopped loving and caring, and working.

His entire life was of helping the less fortunate, including his own mother and dad. Sometimes his wife had to make an appointment to get something she needed done around the house. He was too good for his own good as so many friends told him.

Driving the chemical truck proved to be dangerous. He was the first person in the New Bern area to have the disease called Brainstem Deterioration. Immediately after his retirement he began seven years of declining health which totally disabled him . Billy died on 13 Mar 2007 .He was given a fabulous funeral and parade; his casket was placed on his favorite fire engine that carried him from the funeral home to his grave. The Fire company and the Masonic members gave him eulogy and praise that would have made any hero proud. A brother and a man only in heaven because of Billy's wife, Verna Rose, during his last years, waited on him constantly and completely. Through her Christian love, teaching and witnessing for the Lord and His Kingdom did Billy become prepared to enter heaven with His grace and honor.

23 Jul 1935

Six year old Dallas Jr was on a sport fishing trip with his dad and a party of four on his boat The Tutt. Thirty miles from the dock in Pamlico Sound, a hurricane-like storm without warning hit the area. Four feet high waves knocked the boat around and then the boat engine quit. The boat floundered for a couple of hours. Most of the people in the party became seasick and wondering how much worse the storm could get, and, if the Tutt would take the beating and the rolling. Finally, and just before dark, a freight boat, The Woonsocket, was sighted.

The Woonsocket appeared to be heading their way. There was blessed relief. As the freighter came closer they knew it was coming to rescue them. After pulling beside The Tutt on its leeward side, the adult passengers of The Tutt jumped safely on the Woonsocket as the Tutt was bobbing up and down with the swells of the wild sea. Dallas Sr passed Dallas Jr to a Woonsocket crew member. The big loading doors were closed and the Woonsocket steamed towards the Inland Waterway and Hobucken Coast Guard Station leaving the Tutt and Capt Dallas Sr to wait for a sea tow back to Pamlico. The Coast Guard was already on the way to bring the Tutt and Capt Dallas back to port. The rescued were on dry land at the USCG Station in about two hours. After a thirty minute car ride, they were back in Pamlico Village

The fishing party was over but everyone was glad the Woonsocket and the Coast Guard were available to help them.

1935

James Henry Pittman was born. He is Sadie's brother. He married Alice Kay Gutherie of Morehead City NC while stationed at the Ft Macon US Coast Guard Base. Their sons are James Henry Jr (Jimmy) and Rufus Keith. Keith died in 1985.

6 Jan 1936

Lorena Rawls Quidley died at the USLHS Station at Hobucken NC. Her father and mother were Charles D Rawls and Mary Elizabeth Lewis. Charles Rawls had three wives and three families. Lorena had two sisters: Mary Dell Rawls Bowen in Miami Fl and Maude Isabelle Rawls Slade in Valley Lee Md. Lorena remained in Pamlico NC from marriage to death. Lorena and Maude Isabell visited each other several times in their lifetime.

Maude Isabell and Mary Dell did not see each other for 26 years. Her grandson, Judge John Franklin Slade, flew with her to Miami to see Mary Del when both sisters were in their final years on earth. John said the reunion was very meaningful and emotional for both of the sisters.

Mary Dell was married to Charles Hugh Bowen who was a sports fishing boat owner who took fishing parties out in the ocean to catch fish. They were living in Morehead City NC, where Hugh Bowen was born then they decided to take their family to Miami FL to do the same.

Maude Isabell married John Frank Slade from Whortonsville NC. They had nine children before they left Whortonsville to move to Valley Lee Md. In 1928 there were very few jobs in Whortonsville. John Frank was taking groups from around the country goose hunting to make a living to feed his family. A gentleman from Valley Lee was hunting with John and he was in need of help to run his farms and a rock quary; John and Maude Isabell went to Valley Lee to fulfill his needs. The success story is that John and Isabell become owners of the farms and the rock quary at their benefactor's death.

Maude and John's son, John Frank Jr married Marian Bernadine Gass who came from a family of twelve children. John Frank Jr and Marian had fifteen children.. Many of these children obtained college educations and gained prominence in that area.

John Frank III worked hard and got a law degree and became an attorney. He was elected four times to be a Maryland State Legislator and then became a local Judge. Then, in time he became the District Judge for 15 years. Although now retired from the District Judgeship, he continues to "sit on the bench" several times a week to help with the area's shortage of people who are qualified and available to do the job. He has accomplished a magnificent job of serving the people of southwest Maryland.

John III and Dallas Jr are loving and appreciative third cousins who share grandmother sisters. Ancestry is very important to them. Memories of the time spent with their grandmothers will never leave them.

1936

Katie Lorena Quidley was born at the USLHS Station at Hobucken NC. The delivering physician was Dr John Bonner from Aurora NC. She is the only sister of Dallas Quidley, Jr and she is the only daughter of LHK Dallas E Quidley Sr.

Lorena lost two husbands who died. She raised three children of her husband, Charles James Childress who died 27 Apr 1968. Her next marriage was to Lloyd Donald Leonard who died 1 Nov 2007. The real highlight of her life was the friendship and love she had for Donna MacNevin and her two daughters. Lorena was Nanny to Donna and Ralph MacNevin's children and grandchildren in Naples Florida for over twenty five years. They were her Florida family and they dearly loved her. She was very efficient in managing the home and the children. She spent twenty five years living a wonderful life maintaining their household. The children, Heather and Tiffany, have such deep feeling for Lorena you would think they were a big family of the same blood. Although Lorena can't talk, she shows very much sorrow when she thinks of Donna's death. Donna passed away in 2012 caused by cancer.

Lorena, nicknamed Toni in Florida and Viginia, Boots by her family in NC, has had a hard life with many heartaches and disappointments but she was always able to recover and recoup her happiness. Her faith in God has always brought her back to reality and even in her handicap state, is able to take care of herself. Recovery from her stroke in May 2010 has been another miracle for her by her faith in God and herself.

Lorena, with one hand, has learned to operate a computer, an artificial voice program and a power wheel chair. She will try anything new that will keep her independent. Dallas Jr keeps her pumped up to defend her right of independency. She listens to her big brother. She respects and loves all three of her brothers, Dallas Jr, Elton and Jack Quidley.

Dallas Jr is guardian, Power of Attorney (POA) and administrator for Lorena. She is a miracle in a wheelchair. Just being alive is her only goal and no digression. Her attitude has been excellent.

5 Nov 1936

Capt T D Quidley received a thank you letter from Hardy Nurmsen of New York City. Hardy was writing to thank Capt Quidley for his assistance when he stopped at the Hobucken USLH Station on the last leg of his solo canoe trip from NY thru St Lawrence Seaway, the great lakes and then down the Mississippi River to the Gulf of Mexico, then around Florida and up the Atlantic coast and returned to New York on 11 July, 1936. Most of Hardy's travel was by river or intercoastal waterways. This was a feat no one had done before.

The canoe was equipped for sailing or rowing with little room to eat and sleep, therefore he always appreciated people like Capt Tom who fed him, give him a place to sleep and take a bath. Hardy got a bonus because Capt Tom gave him a money gift for bravery and his accomplishment. That gift took Hardy all the way home to finish his trip and become a hero. Later in life he was recognized by radio and newspaper media. On his trip through North Carolina via the inland waterway Hardy had stopped at the Hobucken USLH Station and spent the night in the home of Capt Thomas D Quidley. He had enjoyed being with Mr Quidley's family, eating at the big dining table with them and was able to take a bath in a real bath tub. It had been a long time since he had such comforts of home. Although the trip was a lot of hard work and sacrifice, Hardy enjoyed his bout with nature and his trip. In the letter to TDQ he showed much appreciation for his assistance and friendship.

He seemed to enjoy the few days with the Quidley family. Capt Tom, an adventurer himself, enjoyed Hardy's and marveled at his spunk and courage.

nov. 5. 1936.
916. E. 232 ST.
BRONX, N.Y. N.Y.

Capt. T. D. Quidley.
Hobucken, N. C.

Dear capt. T. D. Quidley:
                                    Well it has been
long time since I wrote you.
                          I guess I told you already
that I have successfully completed my solo
canoe trip around eastern U. S. A.
              The whole trip took me one year
and seven day and during that time I
paddled and sailed 7200. miles going
through Hudson Rv. Erie Canal, Great Lakes,
Illinois Waterway, Mississippi Rv. Gulf of Mexico,
all the way around Florida, though
through 10.000. islands and keys and up
the Atlantic East Coast back to N.Y.C. where
I arrived at July 11th 1936.
              Had couple radio speeches and
few speeches about my trip in certain
clubs but did not make not a cent money.
But that don't worry me much I had my
trip, met many people and have now

25

friends all over the country.

In Washington D.C. I met your friends Mr. + Mrs. Oliver W. Bailey, nice people.

I have been working already a long time and am used with it again. Conceiving is just a dream now.

Many thanks to your kind cooperation and friendship what made my difficult and hazardous trip much easier and pleasant.

Some time if I happen to be in traveling mood again I might drop in to see you but now I have to close with: Till we meet again, who knows?

as ever your grateful

Hardy.

P.S.

My best regards to all the people I know at Hobucken N.C.

Same.

1 Jun 1937

Lena Mae Quidley and son Dallas Jr (age 8) took a train from Rocky Mount NC to Washington DC. LHK Dallas Quidley Sr met then at Union Station and they drove to Drum Point Lighthouse on the

Chesapeake Bay beach near Solomons MD. The Lighthouse was connected to the beach by a wharf. A great thrill for Lena Mae and Dallas Jr was when the Presidential Yacht Sequoia, with the president and family and friends, took a cruise. They had come down the Patuxent River from Washington DC and while entering the Chesapeake Bay the yacht came close to the Drum Point Lighthouse. The Quidley family waved at the President as he passed. LHK Dallas Quidley Sr always gave the boat a three-toot blow on the big Fog Horn of the lighthouse.

Dallas Jr was eight years old that summer and was very interested in his beach walks, picking up shells. He also found and brought back to the lighthouse many unusual items that had floated to the beach from all over the world. There were items thrown off ships such as a crate of bananas. Dallas Sr quickly buried them on a nearby sand hill telling Jr they were not fit to eat. Other items from beach scavenging were broken oars, cork fishing floats, glass bottles etc which Jr dragged to the lighthouse that summer. There were so many other items that memory does not recall all of them. Lena and Dallas Sr kept him in view even by binoculars if he meandered too far down the beach.

A delightful summer was had by the three. Probably the most delightful and fun summer vacation Dallas Jr ever had. The other three children, Elton, Billy and Lorena remained in Hobucken NC with their aunts, Vicie and Virginia.

Soon after that happy summer, the Drum Point Lighthouse was taken off the pilings and floated on a barge to the town of Solomons Maryland, several miles up the Patuxent River. It is now a part of the Calvert County Park scenery and is open to the public. In 2005 Dallas Jr visited the lighthouse for the first time since 1938.

1 JAN 1939

LHK Dallas Quidley Sr was assigned to the Roanoke Marshes. Dallas Sr bought a home from George Midgett and Arvilla Cudworth Midgett in the Roanoke Island village of Wanchese, NC. Lena was pregnant with her last child to be born, Jack Randall Quidley. She became anemic and needed nurse care and also home care. LHK Quidley's grandmother from Buxton NC, the Hatteras Island midwife and Banker's Nurse came to live with the Quidley family and care for Lena. She took Lena for special medical care and delivery of her soon to be born baby son Jack to Hobucken N C to get more family care if needed. LHK Quidley took a leave of absence from the lighthouse to manage his family in the home while Lena and Grandma were off the Island. get that care. The baby was delivered at the USLHS Station, the home of Capt TD Quidley, after the baby was born and grandma had helped the doctors cure Lena of her anemic blood condition, she started to gain weight and eventually became a healthy person again.

15 Aug 1941

Dallas Jr went to live for the school year in Washington NC with Virginia Q Brown who was living alone while her husband was in the USCG and on a German sub chaser in the North Atlantic Ocean. Dallas Jr completed the seventh grade at Washington Elementary and returned to Manteo Jr High School to do the eighth and ninth grades.

23 Aug 1941

At the end of the summer Dallas Jr was going to spend a few days on Roanoke Marshes Lighthouse with his dad, LHK Dallas Quidley,

Dallas Jr was learning "the ropes" of being a lighthouse keeper and all was "hunky dory". On the second day of the visit LHK Quidley got an emergency message to go to his home in Wanchese because his wife was sick. Dallas Jr begged to stay on the lighthouse while his dad went to their home ashore. Soon after arriving at Wanchese an unexpected north east storm showed up and Dallas Sr could not get back to the lighthouse across Croatan Sound for five days With Dallas Jr charge of the bell and whistle of the lighthouse during this event, it was a night and day mare for his dad.

Junior had plenty of snacks and flavored drink and water. The food storage room had many delicacies such as caned sausage, pork and beans, crackers, cans of various fruit and cookies of all kinds, all were a treat to eat and easy to prepare. Junior was a Boy Scout and had been taught to survive in the woods. The five days went by fast. This last week before school had been a lot of fun. The teenager felt he was fortunate to have no one to supervise him. He had been alone and in charge for almost a week.

15 Nov 1941

Dallas Jr was hospitalized due to an infection and operation on his right big toe. His hospital roommate, William Harvey Williamson from Washington NC had been shot in the right side of his head in a hunting accident. While in that confinement Dallas Jr met the entire Williamson family. Harvey's brother Harold Brian happened to be in the same class at school with Dallas Jr. The Williamson family became Dallas' "Other family." for life. Sixty years later the Williamsons and the Quidleys found that they had been cousins since 1790.

William Harvey Williamson and Harold Brian Williamson were both murdered with guns. Harold was murdered at 21, while serving in the US Army as a Lieutenant, and his brother by a mentally disturbed wife when he was fifty years of age.

1942

Robert Pittman Jr was born. Sadie Pittman Quidley's brother. Bob Graduated from NCSU with a degree in marine biology. After graduation he worked for the NC Department of Conservation. He later became the Assistant Director of the NC Dept of Fisheries. Then, he and his friend, Connel Purvis, former Director of the Dept of Fisheries, who also had left the Dept of Fisheries, bought a seafood company to do blue crab processing. This business lasted many years. When Bob retired from the seafood industry he went to school to become a commercial refrigeration specialist; as an A/C Specialist he opened a new business. His A/C business is doing very well, and he enjoys it so much, that he may never retire again.

12 Jan 1943

Lt John F Kennedy stopped at the Hobucken US Coast Guard Station on the Inland Waterway Canal at Hobucken NC in his PT Boat. He had become sick on the route from his last stop to the Hobucken facility. Dr John Bonner of Aurora was called on the phone. He came to the station to treat Lt Kennedy; Dr Bonner recommended that Lt Kennedy go on to Morehead City on his boat and enter the hospital there. JFK asked the Dr to please travel on the boat with him, but the Dr had too many urgent care patients to leave town at that time.

Seaman 1st Class Thomas Gibbs Quidley, son of Capt T D Quidley, was on duty at the US Coast Guard Station and helped the crew secure the boat to the dock. Many times during Tom's life he told family and friends he had transported Lt Kennedy to the doctor. That could have been to a New Bern or Morehead City hospital. Tom died in 2003 therefore his role in transporting JFK cannot be confirmed.

Dr John Bonner's patient record: John F Kennedy, Age 25, with Intestinal flu, temperature 96, frequent chills. Occupation was US Naval Officer. Home was Massachusetts.

1 FEB 1943

Dallas Quidley Jr had just become fourteen. At fourteen a child could become a worker (get a job) with a work permit. Dallas Jr got his work permit at the Pamlico County Courthouse in Bayboro NC He was super proud. The following Saturday he caught the Seashore Transportation bus in front of his home at Merritt and went to New Bern looking for a job. He got lucky because Copeland-Smith Department Store was hiring young people to be sales clerks, and to help keep the store clean. That was his first job and he was lucky twice, his great aunt Bertha Simpson also worked at Copland-Smith. She knew Nate Thompson who owned The Bootery which was four doors down the street. She realized that Dallas Jr would enjoy working at The Bootery more than at Copeland Smith Company. Aunt Bertha was also a friend of Melissa Carawan Respass, who worked for Mr Thompson. Bertha knew that Melissa would advise and care about a young boy like Dallas Jr. Mr Thompson and Melissa became Dallas Jr's best place to get sales and common sense training.

Two years with The Bootery, the summer job at Cherry Point MCAS, then as Parts Department manager for Lee Motor Sales were the best route a kid could take before entering military service.

1 JUL 1943

LHK Dallas E Quidley Sr resigned from the USLHS in lieu of transfer to the USCG as a Chief CBM), and due to a health condition from the damage to his lungs by fire in 1928. The family moved back to Pamlico County to live in the Ernest Brite home in Merritt NC, six miles from his father, retired Capt Thomas D Quidley.

The family enjoyed living in the Ernest Brite House. It was different from living in small fishing village where homes were close together and kids walked to school. While living at the Brite House the children enjoyed their mother's dad living in the house with them because he made and tended a garden, liked to play games with them, gave the family a horse. He taught them to feed and care for the horse as well as how to ride. Daisy was her name. Dallas Jr liked Daisy because he rode her on long trips to Pamlico and Whortonsville. She never became tired on trips when she could walk an even pace proudly down the dirt roads.

Since the Brite home had been used infrequently in the last ten years a large family of Diamondback rattle snakes had used the barn for their home and the yard for access to other farm yards and barns in the area. The Quidley family often killed these snakes when they were seen crossing the highway after leaving the Brite yard.

When the grandfather selected a stall for Daisy in the barn, he had no idea that snakes had been living in a large stack of old hay in the storage area.. After almost a year of giving Daisy a better stall for comfort and easier feeding, she was bitten by a rattle snake and died before the Vet could answer our phone call for help. Granna Will, a retired farmer, timberman and horse trainer, with the help of friends, cleared the barn of all hay and all snakes. No one missed the snakes. Everyone missed Daisy.

8 Oct 1944

Near Merritt NC on the Florence Road behind the Benson Brite farm there was a Marine Corps bomber crash in the woods. The plane was returning from a long training mission when it ran out of fuel on its approach to Cherry Point Air Station. Margaret Muse of the Benson Brite home remembered a flash she thought was a lightning strike that night; it was a cold and rainy time and the place of the crash was not easy to find. The next morning the US Maine Corp had spotted the crash from the air. The crash site was soon closed off from public view. Somehow word got to Merritt about the crash on the Brite Farm; Dallas Jr and his brothers were there before the site was closed to outsiders.. It was a bad smelling place. There were no large parts of crew members or the airplane, except the tail section was hanging in a large pine tree. Five young men had died for their country. The crash site should never be abandoned and those five young men forgotten.

1 Sep 1945

Dallas E Quidley Jr met Sadie Rae Pittman who had moved from Lukens NC to Oriental NC during the last year. She was a Junior and he was a Senior at Oriental High School. They were married on 7 July 1950 at MGuire AFB Chapel in Wrightstown NJ.

1 Jun 1946

Dallas Jr started his summer job at the Cherry Point Maine Corps Air Station as a student training employee. The job was to provide furniture and equipment for the military homes of families living on the air base. Mr Cyrus Gaskins was in charge of the summer team of students. His kindness and understanding and his superior techniques of handling a bunch of young boys was a great help to Dallas and all others involved. The few months went by quickly; they all made a few bucks to help them get ready for school. The important part of the job was that each of the boys had some wonderful memories to last a life time.

Dallas was probably more fortunate in the learning process than most of the boys. While helping one young Marine family prepare for leaving one of the homes, he met a 24 year old LT who took an interest in Dallas and explained his military service and what it meant to him. The Lt was soon to depart from the Marine Corps for college.

The war was ending but the young marine had worried about the future of America and what young people like Dallas Jr would be facing. He had said it would come more quickly than most people realized. He really was warning Dallas to be prepared for military service which he thought would begin again within five years.

The young marine's advice started a patriotic thought process that would prepare Dallas to understand the world, the politics of the USA mixed with the thrust of communist aggression to take over the world. In three years Dallas felt the effects of the young Marine's prediction. Communist Aggression started the war talk, the preparation for war and the attack on South Korea by North Korea all instigated by China and Russia. The new Cold war was really going to be a hot one. Dallas was glad he had known what to expect and how to cope with the Lt's predictions.

Nov 1946

DEQ Jr, then 16, hitched a ride from Merritt to Oriental with Butch Hardison from Arapahoe NC. The car was already full of boys. Dallas sat on the right side on the front seat. He was a somewhat afraid of Butch's driving but found a thrill to feel the speed while passing other cars. Butch was blowing the horn at people he recognized walking or driving.

As they approached the big curve entering Oriental Butch lost control of the car and it began rolling. It rolled three times and each time Dallas Jr thought to himself, "when this thing quits rolling I can get out of the side window." He had no seat belt so he just grabbed the bottom of the seat and held on tight during the rolls. When all four wheels stayed on the ground, he knew it was time to go through that window. It was a small hole because the top of the car had been bent in each time the car rolled, He was lucky that he was a skinny kid. His broken rib was taped and he got a few aspirin for the soreness to come. Also, he got a good lecture from the Doctor who was a friend of his dad and granddad. Dr James Purdy had brought Dallas Jr into the world sixteen years earlier.

23 May 1947 Dallas Jr Graduated from Oriental HS. He was Vice President of his class. His cousin Paul Carraway Brady was President.

1947

Thomas Bradford Pittman was born. He is a brother of Sadie Pittman. Tom graduated from East Carolina University with a degree in business and finance. He has spent a career in sales. He retired in 2012. He married Nancy Williams and they have two beautiful daughters one of whom is a teacher and the other is a nurse.

2 Aug 1948

Dallas E Quidley Jr Joined the United States Air Force

1 Nov 1948

Dallas began work with Lt Robert Laden, the administrator of base Non-Appropriated Funds. The office was in the Base Gymnasium. The Gymnasium was large and it also housed the Base Service Club. PFC Quidley was also a B 29 crew member. This dual job each Thursday was for flight training, and Lt Robert Laden was the pilot. The B 29 during peace time training had a crew of six. Dallas was the right scanner which would have been a right tail gunner if and when the plane was activated for war.

Lt Robert Laden was the first AF Officer Dallas had come to know. Lt Laden saw that Dallas was trained more than he had been taught in basic military training. Dallas considered the accounting and the crew training by Lt Laden so important that he gives a whole lot of credit for his happy and successful career in the USAF to his pilot and friend.

Dallas will never forget his first ride on the B 29 to NC and back to NJ with one Ground Control Approach landings (GCA) at Andrews AFB in Washington DC. PFC Quidley remembered well that one of the right engines developed an oil leak between Andrews AFB and McGuire AFB. He saw thru his round bubble window the constant dripping of oil from the very large Pratt and Whitney engine. An emergency landing was prepared for by the McGuire AFB Fire & Rescue Department. Flashing red and blue lights on the runway greeted B 29 Number 1813. It was a relief PFC Quidley had when the plane's wheels came down and soon touched the runway with grace and dignity. Dallas Jr thanked the Good Lord for another wonderful day.

Several training flights later the crew met at the plane soon after daylight. It had snowed the night before. The snow plow was still working on the mile long runway. In starting the engines for warm up, one of the engines did not want to crank normally and a mechanic had to come and do his thing. After all four engines had been started and the snow cleared from the wings, we hustled down the runway; Almost instantly the plane was over the New Jersey coastline.

In the first twenty minutes after taking off they were still over southern NJ with snow on the ground below. Lt Robert Laden from the cockpit, turned Dallas' radio on so he could hear Arthur Godfrey's morning show. The pilot had control of communication equipment on board the big aircraft. Dallas had never heard of Arthur Godfrey but he still recollects that beautiful morning well. That day's training flight took them to the New Bern NC area and then over Pamlico County so that PFC Dallas Quidley could see his home and wave at his mom who did not even know her son was in the plane flying above. She was hanging bed sheets on the clothes line. Later when he asked her on the phone if she saw him fly overhead, she said she thought it was one of the planes preparing to land at Cherry Point Marine Air Base across the Neuse River. That was a disappointment.

On Cpl Quidley's last flight on the big bird it was early spring. Arriving at the plane before anyone else, Dallas found time to sit and relax on the grassed area beside the runway; With some time to spare, he found a patch of clover. He searched the big patch and found six clovers with the lucky number of leaves. Each member of the crew on the flight that day had a four leaf clover for good luck.

The trip was uneventful as the superfortress carried the training crew on another pre-war training flight. This flight was to the Great Lakes area and then around Chicago and back to NJ. Quidley did not recall a landing or GCA. (Ground Control Approach is when the landing is completely controlled by people on the ground). From Illinois the flight continued on to McGuire AFB.

Lt Laden was one of the best of B 29 pilots and could handle any situation that might fly his way. The crew was always a cheerful bunch having fun being real Airmen. That was just like their Air Force recruiter had told them it would be,

Robert Laden was a friend to Dallas who at that time thought he was a long, long way from home. Bob's wife Mary and three year old daughter Alexis were like family to the young man that was also new in their lives.

Dallas developed many wonderful friendships from the beginning of his military life. Many of these friends, plus The Lord's blessings, helped him and his family for the remainder of his life. Many different employers with a wide range of educations and professions gave Dallas a sense of urgency to study and learn and to improve while helping others.

I Jun 1949

Because the entire Bomb Wing was being moved
and most all flying personnel being relocated
somewhere else, Cpl Quidley and PFC Rabik were
offered the chance to stay at McGuire AFB. The
transferring Bomb Wing at the time did not have a
Chaplain Department; the Chaplains also remained
at McGuire AFB.

Dec 1949

McGuire AFB became a ghost town after the
Bomb Wing left the Air Base. Dallas and Willis
Rabik were the only occupants in the WW2
barracks formerly called the Wing Barracks. There
were four of these buildings alike in a circle with
a latrine (shower and toilet building) in the center
with covered, heated and concrete floored corridors
from each of the barracks to the latrine. This was
snow season in New Jersey therefore the heat, the
corridors and well-constructed frame buildings
were appreciated. Ceilings with exposed rafters
became very useful to Dallas' plan to scare Willis
out of being scared. In their barrack the bunks
(single beds) were headed towards the non-window
wall with a long shelf over the full length of each
person's area. There was space for a bed and one
night stand. The shelf had a clothes hanging rod
for all hanging clothes. Occupants kept their folded

and personal clothing and valuables locked in duffle bags between the head of the bed and the wall. The exposed rafters above the beds made it easy to throw a long rope over the rafter and hide the rope behind the clothes hanging under the shelf. In the dimly lighted room an unsuspecting person would not see the rope pulling action, but would hear the sounds of movements caused by the primitive mechanical system. It had to work.

PFC Willis Rabik came into the barracks to sleep. He pulled back the covers and quickly but quietly jumped in his bed. He just knew that Dallas was sleeping because he could hear him breathing, maybe snoring. After he had gotten settled and warm, ready for sleep, Willis heard a light tap on the floor behind his bed. It sounded to him like his duffle bag was jumping up and down leaving the floor and then dropping to the floor. After several minutes of this, the annoyance in the mind of Willis became a miserable fear of a ghost in the barracks. After all, there were several crew members who had once slept there during WW2 who had died in air battles overseas and they might have returned to their old quarters to visit. Willis' hard breathing could have been heard by most everyone in the big room had there been anyone there but he and Dallas. He was allowed to suffer fear only a few more minutes before Dallas burst out of bed and calmly said "it is only me. You should not be afraid." Then again, with only a few more nights before both airmen were to depart the old barracks, Willis was fear tested again.

This time a simpler scene was set up. Willis had finished his shower and "whistled back" to his room in his sleeping clothes. He had his dirty clothes ready to deposit in a clean large special bag behind his bed. He felt and found the bag, opened the top of it and a skinny hand grabbed the young airman's hand and yanked on it. Willis yelled loudly and ran down the hall of the barrack with Dallas behind him telling him, "Look, it is only little old me." It was instantly a laughing matter to both of them.

The next and last scare trick came after Willis had time to think about being so foolish. Cpl Quidley and PFC Rabik knew their time of being roommates was ending and, it had been good friends helping each other to survive and improve. Worse times were ahead. Willis still showed a little sign of fear at nights in strange places. This was the last time Dallas would have to scare the daylights into him.

The time and scene were the same except the devil, Dallas, devised a new fear contraption. The good soul, Willis, came in from his nightly shower and in the dark as usual, got into his bed and covered up fully. This time a wire clothes hanger, straight as could be, had a bend at one end making it a hook to bring things to the puller. The hook end was fastened to the outer blanket of Willis' bed covering, Dallas, the acting ghost, began pulling the covering off the fearful sleeping giant. The Sleeping giant, Willis was a big person, and he yanked harder and pulled Cpl Quidley off his feet. They both laughed. The experiment had ended. Willis was not afraid again.

10 Jan 1950

Chaplain Arthur Brenner and his wife Trudy invited Dallas to accompany them to the Idlewild Airport (now Kennedy) in New York to pick up their new son who was flying in from Germany. The new son, Peter Rolf Brenner was an adopted child coming from one of Hitler's mistakes. Peter was born from the mandated marriage of two super German people whom Hitler thought would bring about a new super race of youth for his exploitation of the world. Peter has proved that the intelligence part of the plan was correct.

After Hitler was gone, the children came up for adoption and only the best family situation was allowed to have one of the children. Arthur and Trudy got Peter and he grew up to be a super young man joining the US Navy. He also became a Chaplain. He did not remain in the military service but after his military service he took a Methodist Church in Michigan where he is today. He has a family and is enjoying the American way.

Feb 1950

A young US Army Sgt with three years of service behind him, who had been stationed in Japan for a couple of years, decided he wanted to be transferred to the front lines of South Korea. The Korean War was soon to start raging after a slow start, therefore this dedicated brave GI from Rocky Mount NC soon found himself on guard at the border between South Korea and North Korea. While on guard duty one night he was captured and he became a Prisoner of War (POW). His parents in Rocky Mount learned of his capture in several days, they were devastated. That was the last anyone heard from Sgt Charles Brantley for three long years until he was released to the Army.

A few weeks after his release from being a POW for three years, he was returned to his family in Rocky Mount. He returned to his mother in deteriorated condition. His mother met him with his medical aide at the train station. The mother did not recognize him and when she found out that it was her son, she fainted. After many months of medical treatment and recuperation Charles became an Army recruiter in Rocky Mount NC.

Six years from home had changed greatly for Charles; his dad had died, his mother had remarried and his siblings had become grown. It was after he became an Army recruiter that Dallas Quidley met him and worked with him for two years. Sgt Quidley was the Air Force Recruiter and he was the Army Recruiter. They worked together and became good friends. Charles did not like to talk about his Army life in Korea, but Dallas found out from other sources that he was a real hero from many acts while in the POW camps. His POW group was marched several hundred miles from the border area to deep inside North Korea. On that march one such heroic act occurred when a buddy on the march became sick or was injured and could not walk, Charles carried him the remainder of the death march on his back. He also did not give in to the unrelenting hateful demands of the hate driven guards and their supervisors. He remained strong and protected others as long as he could.

When Sgt Brantley finally retired from the Army on disability, he became a US Postman in his home city. He enjoyed being at home and was a dedicated postman remembering the good and bad old days.

Dallas was proud to serve with him for that short period.

6 Jun 1950

Sgt Dallas Quidley went on short leave of absence to North Carolina. He wanted to be with his family and Sadie before the wedding on 7 July. This was a trip mainly to talk about the scheduled wedding. A friend driving to Florida gave him a ride to NC. For the return trip from NC to NJ he was able to catch a flight by military plane from Cherry Point MCAS to Anacostia Station, DC. There, he got lucky and found a ride on an old C47 directly back to McGuire AFB. The C47 was an old cargo plane that did not have ordinary plane seats, but had built in metal benches on each side of the plane. It had been used for paratrooper drops in WW2.

An older looking USAF Major sitting beside Dallas told Dallas he felt sick and needed to lay down on the bench seat or the floor. Dallas went to the nearby parachute stack and quickly grabbed a parachute to use as a pillow for the sick man. In the rush Dallas got the handle mixed up with the "cord" (to open). The chute bloomed open and partially filled the plane. Instead of a parachute for a pillow the sick man got two folded Air Force jackets bundled together. After hearing the commotion over the opened chute, the Flight Steward showed up who informed Sgt Quidley that the plane only carried enough chutes for each passenger to have one. Dallas told him that he would repack it if it became necessary and would wear it. The Steward, also a Sgt, tells Dallas he will inform the Pilot. Nothing else was said and the plane landed at McGuire in about forty minutes. Dallas has many times since then thought "what if?"

7 JUL 1950

Dallas & Sadie were married at McGuire AFB Chapel near Wrightstown NJ. The ceremony was performed by Chaplain (Capt) Arthur Emil Kalk Brenner and Rev Thomas Wright, a local Methodist minister. The bride was given into marriage by Colonel Edward S Tate, McGuire AFB Commander. The bride's father and mother could not be present due to ill health and the long distance from Oriental NC to McGuire AFB. The marriage was blessed also by Chaplain (Lt Col) Lucien A Madore who attended the wedding and the reception, and provided the reception facility. It was a beautiful reception at the Catholic Church Family Center in Brown's Mill NJ.

A beautiful wedding cake was a gift from Mrs Peggy Harris and the Staff of the McGuire AFB Service Club.

Dallas's mother, brother (Jack) and sister (Lorena) attended the wedding. His father was unable to attend the service or the reception.

As man and wife Dallas and Sadie lived at 216 Parker Road in Lakewood NJ. The home was about twenty miles from McGuire AFB. Oakley M Parker owned the home and lived there also. Their rent was paid by feeding Mr Parker and keeping a part of the house clean. They enjoyed the beautiful old farm house with a seven acre yard. Oakley was a retired high school teacher living alone on the property. It was once a part of the John D Rockefeller Ocean County Estate. Oakley's dad worked for John D and had purchased, or was given, the seven acres. Oakley had a sister, Dr Z Rita Parker, also not married. She was Chief Psychiatrist at Belview Hospital in New York City. She was known around the world, and was a leader in her field. She owned an island in Maine for vacation and get away. Thru her we met many celebrities.

Dr Parker was a psychiatrist to several Hollywood persons. She also kept some of the Rockefeller family members tuned up. One of her most notable celebrity clients was Ms Spring Byington of Hollywood and New York. During her last days of life she visited Dallas Jr's parents in Meritt NC. Dallas Jr appreciated Dr Parker's interest in his family and he enjoyed the love of her own family.

Dallas and Sadie communicated with Oakley Parker from the time they left his home until he died in

Feb 1977. After Dallas retired from the US Air Force he transported Mr Parker from his home in Lakewood NJ to Fort Lauderdale Florida beginning the annual trip on each 14th of December; then the following 15th of April Dallas would pick him up in Florida and take him back to his home in New Jersey. There was always a week of visiting the Quidley home in New Bern both going to Florida and returning to NJ.

17 Nov 1950

On this date a dear friend Capt Robert Laden and his B29 crashed at Johnson AFB near Tokyo Japan after being hit by three MIG 15s. The B29 (# 1823) had been on a bombing mission over North Korea and the MIGs tried to shoot them down over the Sea of Japan. One engine was out and there were many controls not functioning; It would be a hard landing even with three engines still going. But Capt Laden was determined to save his crew and he tried everything he could. He circled the Air Base several times to use up as much fuel as possible to lessen the chance of fire and explosion; he watched as two more engines went out in his final approach Even with very little power he got within glide distance to the runway. It appears that anything bad that could happen did so during the most critical time of the flight. The plane hit the ground one hundred yards short of the touch down area. It was broken into two pieces.

The pilot, Capt Laden, and three other officers in the cockpit died instantly. The precious lives of the tail crew members were saved and they were able to crawl out of the tail section thankful to God for all his mercy. Had Dallas stayed with that crew at McGuire AFB he too would have been saved. He would have been in the tail section.

Feb 1951

A friend, religious mentor and Church Leader Arthur E K Brenner had less time in the Air Force than Cpl Dallas Quidley . Chaplain Brenner had graduated from Temple University in Philadelphia PA with a doctorate in Divinity and Counseling;

he was the Protestant Chaplain and Dallas was his assistant for the past year. Arthur was under Lt Col Lucien A Madore and Dallas was under the supervision of Chaplain Brenner. Both Chaplain Brenner and Cpl Quidley reported to Ch Madore. Besides being Base Chaplain he was the Catholic priest to all Catholics on the Base. His Catholic assistant was PFC Willis Rabik and Willis and all other Chaplain Assistants reported to Cpl Dallas Quidley for supervision and military training. Everyone knew their jobs, their military duties and respected each other. Since there were many problems associated with the military and their families, every chaplain was selected to serve only if they had specialized training in solving emotional and military problems. Arthur E K Brenner had a better education in psychology than anyone else. Dallas Quidley, a waterman and student from Eastern NC was where he needed to be, with a psychologist, a preacher, a priest and teacher. His on the job education began to move ahead fast.

The Air Force problem for and with Arthur was that he had not realized yet that in the military you were an officer but a chaplain first, After that a minister and a Christian person had to learn to accept the rights of all other denominations of all other faiths. He loved the Lord, he loved to preach and teach and he was a good example of Jesus Christ. He brought to the Lord as many of his faith as he could both military and civilian. The military commander's main requirement was for all Chaplains to teach, preach and assure that all members were spiritually tuned. Arthur was about to learn to be a great Chaplain the hard way.

One of Cpl Quidley's required tasks was being the Religious Supply Clerk. As such he did a weekly inventory of all items in the supply room. He started to notice that the Catholic Service Guides were flying off the shelves by the case. These being gifts from local Catholic Authority, Cpl Quidley asked Chaplain Madore if he knew where they were going. He could not understand the added use, and insisted that his requirement had not changed.

Then, the next day after that discussion, he saw Chaplain Brenner with a case of books heading to the coal fired furnace near his office. A closer look and he saw books burning on top of the hot coals. He confronted Chaplain Brenner and told him, "Please don't do that again." No apology or response was heard. The same event happened about a week later. That time he told the Chaplain that one more time and he would be reported to the Catholic Chaplain who was also the Base

Chaplain. In a few days it happened again. Dallas told Arthur he was on his way to make the report. Arthur told Dallas he did not need an Assistant any longer. Dallas went in the Chapel. He sat and prayed for Arthur and himself. He then slowly meandered to the Base Chaplain's office

Upon arrival at Chaplain Madore's office Dallas was told to relax and that Chaplain Brenner had already been there. Chaplain Brenner had explained what he had done and apologized to Father Madore. Chaplain Madore said he had already called and given the Command Chaplain in NY the story; he said he needs an Assistant and wants you transferred to his office within ten days. Sgt Quidley was told to go home and tell his wife, Sadie, to get their household items ready for shipment to Stewart AFB NY.

Chaplain Madore also said," You and Sadie can go on to Newburgh and find you a place to live." This they did after telling Arthur and Trudy goodbye. Both couples were sad because of this firey episode.

1 Mar 1951

Upon arriving at Newburg NY to begin work at Stewart AFB, Dallas and Sadie found an apartment at 310 Grand Street facing the Hudson River. It was a basement apartment but it was a dream place to this newly married couple. The owner of the home, Celia Winstone, occupied the first floor and her daughter, Ruby, and her family, had the two top floors.

When being introduced by Mrs Winstone to her daughter and family, Dallas realized he had just read in the New York Times that his and Sadie's new neighbors were international celebrities. Ruby was Mrs Luis Rudolpho Padilla-Nervo, wife of the new and 5th President of the United Nations. They had a seven year old son, Adrian. Dallas and Sadie got to know the Winstones and Nervos very well in the months to follow.

President Nervo, prior to this title, had been Ambassador from Mexico to Germany, England and the USA. He had graduated from college as a Medical Doctor. He also had a Doctorate in Business and Law. After his term as President of the United Nations he then became Secretary of State of Mexico. In Newburg the Nervos had four maids and two chauffeurs. They had only one Stretch Limo and no cars because Ruby did not drive. Ruby and Adrian liked Dallas's Henry J better than the limo.

Dallas enjoyed making model airplanes for Adrian, also fixing his motorized play car. However, the wooden box with wheels, being pushed by Dallas, was much more fun for Adrian than his entire room of electric toy trains running on a custom built "train city" track.

Sadie and Dallas will never forget the day that Ruby asked them to take her and Adrian to a farm in the country. She had seen a newspaper advertisement of a farm about fifty miles west of Newburgh that took in special guests to live on a real farm. It had sounded exactly what Adrian might like; he could see all of the animals and play with them. Ruby was a large person and always had difficulty getting into the Henry J, but this day she seemed to make out fine in entering and exiting. The trip to the farm was pleasant and we had fun chatting, They found the farm easily. After a bumpy ride down a rock road they came to the farm house. It was a rustic complex containing the house surrounded by barns, an outhouse and tractor sheds. You could see horses, cows and a few pigs in a pen.

Ruby quickly got out of the car alone and began a trek to the front door of the house. Dallas was fairly certain he could see her taking in deep breaths (such as smelling) , and that she had already concluded that the farm experience was not for herself or Adrian. Dallas thought at first she might have robbed a bank when she said "Get out of here fast". She found the odors of the farm to be repulsive. The next stop was in the next village where she saw a sign on a fancy updated Colonial Home with a sign out front that said "Rooms to Rent with Restaurant and a Swimming Pool." She got checked in. Ruby insisted that Luis would send for them when he got back from a UN meeting in the City. Sadie and Dallas enjoyed the trip to the farm and will never forget Adrian's disappointment that he could not stay at the farm.

They also never forgot the Mexican maids who sneaked out of the house to meet their boyfriends when they returned they sometimes found the elevator up to their room was locked. Ruby never found out that Dallas and Sadie let the maids go through their apartment to gain entrance to the building and their quarters.

At the end of his term at the United Nations the Nervos went back to Mexico City to live. Sadie and Dallas received invitations to attend the new home Open House and the 50th Wedding celebration. They even invited Dallas and Sadie to come to Mexico to live. Ruby and Luis both passed away during the 1970s in Mexico City. The Quidleys have not heard from Adrian in many years

1 JUN 1951

Due to the escalating war in Korea, Chaplain Arthur Brenner received orders to go to a front line Air Base in South Korea. His career as a worthy military chaplain became known there for his many baptisms in Korean rivers and streams.

Somehow the news media decided to give him full coverage of his religious activities in Korea. He worked diligently with Air Force troops, the US Army Troops and Korean Army Troops. In his spare time he built an orphanage to take care of the Korean War orphans. He even built a women's wig factory to give employment to families, and to provide funds to operate the orphanage. When he had spent his required time in the war zone he asked to remain in Japan. He wanted to give his wife and son a chance to be with him and enjoy the beautiful Far East. Dallas' job as an assistant to the Command Chaplain in the Far East Air Forces, Col Terrence P Finnegan, Arthur's application got quick and special attention. It was approved and Chaplain Finnegan told SSgt Quidley to call Chaplain Brenner and inform him to tell his wife Trudy, in the US, to get ready to move to Yakota AFB. Chaplain Brenner and Dallas were happy to hear each other and to renew old friendships. When the Brenners got settled in their home on Yakota AB, Dallas spent some time with them and marveled at how Peter Rolf had grown. The Brenners and Dallas had picked him up at the airport in NY as a six year old child. and now he was ten.

Chaplain (Major) Arthur Brenner became a full Colonel in six years and then several years later. Chaplain (Colonel)

Dallas Edward Quidley Jr.

Terrence P Finnegan became Chief of Air Force Chaplains as a Lt General in Washington DC.

4 Nov 1951

Dallas Jr Departed for Japan & Korea in a P51 from Cherry Pt to DC. His dad, Dallas Sr, had a friend who was a squadron commander at Cherry Point MCAS who flew an experimental Double P 51. This was two P51 bodies, each with a cockpit, two tail sections and two engines. It was an unusual sight. Sgt Quidley could talk with the pilot on intercom and wave at him in the other cockpit, but they did not share the same heat. Dallas said it was a cold ride. Anyway, Dallas Jr got a free ride in a super fighter plane from Cherry Point Air Station to Andrews AFB Md. From Andrews AFB he caught a quick shuttle to Idlewild Field (now Kennedy). After a short wait he boarded his fight on a DC 4 to Chicago Il, where he transferred to another DC 4 (United Airlines Flight # 611) for Denver, Salt Lake and Oakland CA.

5 Nov 1951

At about one a.m. aboard flight # 611 to Oakland CA via Chicago Il, Sgt Quidley woke up to find the DC 4 circling Denver Airport with the pilot preparing to land in a snow storm. In just a few minutes the plane was again climbing and the pilot announced that they were heading to Salt Lake City where it would be safe to land. Half hour later the sound of a engine sputtered and # 4 right engine cut off . Then # 3 on the right stopped. Passenger worry hit everyone on board the plane; there was almost dead silence. Everyone knew there were only two engines running and they were on one side of the airplane. Although a bit distressing to hear, the passengers were glad to hear the pilot's voice this time. He said that a wheels–up landing in the snow would be necessary because it was impossible to keep the runway at Cheyenne AFB completely clear of snow. The pilot told the passengers on the intercom that it would be a safe landing, not to worry, that he had been thru this same procedure before. Although most all passengers were calm, there were many who prayed aloud which calmed the meeker people. A Catholic priest was praying louder than the others; his prayer made sense and that was extra calming.

Shortly everyone was anticipating a hard bump and a long slide in the snow, however all of a sudden the snow was going over the wings like dust. The snow was a powder-like snow and it had cushioned the impact. The plane had come in smoothly and straight, and it soon stopped sliding. The soft snow had slowed the plane to a gentle stop. It was a beautiful sight to see the doors of the plane open and there were snow weasels (multi passenger snow mobiles) waiting to whisk passengers and crew through the snow to a motel in Cheyenne. What a trip that was!!!!

7 Nov 1951

Sgt Quidley boarded another plane going to Salt Lake City Utah & San Francisco CA. The stop at Salt Lake City Utah was a short one but the beautiful scenes Dallas saw during landing and takeoff were exhilarating. The Great Salt Lake with the sun hitting it that morning was like a bed of diamonds.

When Dallas arrived at the port in San Francisco he found that a Telegraph message had been sent to the Embarkation Office which said

"Please excuse Sgt Dallas E Quidley Jr for late arrival to your organization yesterday. The delay was due to a mechanical failure on Flight 611 from Chicago to Oakland.

20 Nov 1951

UNITED AIR LINES

MAINTENANCE BASE
P. O. BOX 3000
SOUTH SAN FRANCISCO, CALIFORNIA

November 5, 1951

Commanding Officer
2353d PP5, 2349th PP6.
Camp Stoneman
Pittsburg, California

Dear Sir:

Please be advised that S/Sgt. Dallas E. Gundley, AF 14282461 and Pfc George W. Rocher, AF 14371705 boarded our Flight 611 on November 4, 1951 in Chicago, Illinois for San Francisco, Calif. The scheduled arrival time of this flight in San Francisco would normally be 4:50 A.M. November 5, 1951. However said flight was delayed enroute on account of adverse weather conditions and mechanical difficulties. S/Sgt. Gundley and Pfc Rocher were subsequently accommodated on the first available flight to San Francisco, arriving 5:00 P.M., November 5, 1951.

Yours very truly
Dewey Lowe
Passenger Agent

Departed San Francisco CA on the USS Gen Mitchell (Tap 114) for Yokohama, Tokyo and eventually several trips to South Korea.

26 Nov 1951

Dallas crossed the International Date Line at Latitude 34 Degrees at 1400 hours.

2 Dec 1951

Dallas saw Japanese coastline at 1900 hours. After the ship landed and all passengers had gotten dust on their shoes, Dallas left Yokohama Japan for Tokyo Japan at 1800 hours

4 Dec 1951

Sgt Dallas Quidley was assigned to the Far East Air Forces Office in the Meiji Building directly across the street from the Imperial Palace Grounds. He was to be an assistant to Chaplain (Colonel) Terrence P Finnegan (later in career became a Lt General and the Chief of Air Force Chaplains). When Chaplain Finnegan's Hollywood Entertainment friends came to the Far East for troop shows they would stop by the office to see Chaplain Finnegan. Their pilgrimage visits were how Dallas was able to meet Bob and Delores Hope and a few other celebrities.

S Sgt Quidley's main job in the FEAF Office was to read, correct and forward to the next of kin messages concerning their killed, injured or missing relatives in the war zone (South Korea). It was necessary to read all daily reports regarding aircraft accidents, on-AFB accidents, hospitalized military and civil service employees in the Far East Air Forces (Okinawa, Korea, Japan, etc). Also these reports covered the sighting of POW personnel (or word from intelligence sources on their fate).

5 Dec 1951

SSgt Quidley moved into the New Kaijo Building 7th floor apartment, with Marvin Ulrich, Maurice Smestad, John Chumley and James C Reno as roommates. The New Kaijo building was in downtown Tokyo across from the Imperial Palace Plaza.

The dormitory building was used by Meiji Industries during WW2. The building had a solid floored roof which made exercising, running and sun bathing a daily jaunt. Here was a health nut's dream. Each dormitory room had a five guest capacity.. There were two bath rooms in each unit.. One large dining room on the first floor fed all occupants of the building. On the top floor there was a snack bar and large living room for relaxing. This room had facilities for hobbies and music.

This group of friends was able to continue their college and technical studies while stationed in Japan. With John Chumley, to become a world famous artist, all in his group got much technical instruction and with excellent photography training. John had been trained at the Ringling School of Art in Sarasota FL; He was a real artist and enjoyed photography as well. He made charcoal and pencil sketches of each of us while we were housed and worked together, but he would never give us a copy. He said that he was taught not to give away any of his works prematurely. He seemed to know he would be famous someday. John died of cancer in 1985.

JAN 1952

While on duty with the USAF in Tokyo Dallas was in his office on the seventh floor of the Meiji Building when a severe earthquake struck. The building shook, the doors and windows squeaked. The chandelier lights in the offices swung like wind chimes. His office chair with rollers slammed against the nearest wall; everything moved but the quake was over in a matter of seconds. The fright subsided but the memory remains. Dallas' thoughts during the quake, in this new experience were, "I miss the hurricanes of NC because when the wind blows hard, at least the ground stands still." After that earthquake several others were felt but did not cause as much damage.

10 Feb 1952 W Daniels (CW) came to Tokyo to visit from Okinawa. Dallas and his roommates showed C W the Tokyo sights, and accompanied him on trips to the Ginza Strip where one could find anything made in the Far East. Everything was there from pearls and colored diamonds to clothing, art ware and inexpensive "junk". C W Daniels had a fabulous vacation from the Island of Okinawa. Dallas noted that he had actually matured more than himself since seeing him at McGuire AFB. Dallas did not see his neighbor from Merritt NC as a young person again. CW had retired from operation and ownership of a household appliance store in Virginia. He died of cancer in a few years after retirement. CW is buried in the Trent FWB Church Cemetery in Merritt NC.

11 Mar 1952

Lt Harold Bryan Williamson was killed (murdered) at Ft Hood TX. A disgruntled, probably mentally disturbed, eighteen year old Army Private wanted to get out of the military service. His weak mind told him that if he shot an Officer of the Day (OD), the Army would discharge him immediately. Without bullets for his issued rifle, he packed the barrel with gun powder and inserted a barrel cleaning rod down the barrel chamber. The Soldier, in a mess tent on the Army Post, waited for his OD target, and Lt Harold Williamson happened to be OD on that fateful day.

In reviewing the recent murder event at Ft Hood where 13 people were shot to death by a traitor Army Major, not a true American or of the intelligence and value of Lt Harold Williamson. There were very few similarities. The recent case at Ft Hood is a disgrace to the US Army and the USA.

Harold's death and the thirteen recently killed could have been avoided had the Army been allowed to control their enlistee quality and nationality. Lt Harold Williamson could have become a real asset to his country. Harold's family and friends are still remembering a very promising young man who had graduated with honors from NC State University as a Cadet Colonel in the College ROTC, and he also had grand musical, engineering and military talents. Since Dallas Jr was overseas in Japan at the time of Harold's death he was represented by Dallas Jr's grandfather, T D Quidley, at the funeral. Harold's tragedy remains very depressing.

2 Apr 1952

Dallas climbed Mt Fujiama in Central Japan with roommates and dear friends John Chumley, Marvin Ulrich, Maurice Smestad and James C Reno. On this spring day the weather was beautiful until you reached the snow cap. Each of the Team photographed and enjoyed the many changing scenes. The climb was another delightful memory of beautiful Japan.

April 1952

Dallas Edward Quidley III was born at 0300 hours at the US Naval Hospital Cherry Point Marine Corps Air Station NC. See the description in his birth announcement, his USAF assignment to Silicon Valley CA and Sgt Quidley's arrival from overseas.

1 May 1952

Communist May Day riots happened in downtown Tokyo. Sgt Quidley saw very much damage done that day by fools listening to a foolish ideology. The crowd came rushing from East Tokyo on Imperial Palace Drive in a planned and coordinated pattern. The group had the appearance of ignorance plus evil.

Sgt Quidley and the other office staff members watched from office windows on the 7th floor of the Meiji Building. The wild crazy, fanatical crowd burned cars, pulled down and destroyed street signs. They made very scary screams and mechanical noises. This is the same building where General Douglas McArthur had his headquarters at the end of WW2. Had this motley coward group done this when he was in that building, World War Two would have restarted that day.

9 JUN 1952

While on a flight to K47 (Korean AFB) an aircraft was damaged by enemy fire. Dallas was on Air Force duty that day. SSgt Quidley was on casualty assistance and reporting business.

9 OCT 1952

While assigned to the 315th Air Division in Fuchu Japan, he moved out in the country 15 miles from Tokyo. This is a very quiet country, non-airport AFB Base. Being stationed there was truly like living in the real Japan as you see life in travel brochures.

Apr 1953

SSgt Dallas Quidley promoted to Technical Sgt

11 Apr 1953 departed Japan on USS Mann at 1800

27 Apr 1953 Dallas arrived USA San Francisco at 1000

1 May 1953

Dallas was reunited with Sadie and Ed at 0300 in Rocky Mt, NC. Missed Ed's first birthday by 3 hours. Sgt Quidley knew his son would be a mechanical person of some kind. Ed and his mom had been waiting at the hotel for their returning loved one. Ed woke before his dad the next morning. He had time to search his dad's luggage; he found a wind up Baby Ben alarm clock which fascinated him. By the time Sgt Quidley got out of bed Ed had completely dismantled the clock and piled the pieces on the floor to show his dad. Sadie, by way of many photos and lots of talk, had son Ed knowing his dad and immediately called him "dado".

Jan 1954

Harold Anthony Quidley was born at the USAF Hospital at Lake Charles AFB LA. Harold was welcomed from day one by his brother Ed. When Harold got home from the hospital and was in his crib, Ed brought all his toys and put them in the crib with Harold.

A few years paased when Dallas was at work and Sadie was in the yard, Harold got his first haircut by his brother Ed. Ed had decided that Harold with his long hair had been called a little sister too long. Ed was tired of Harold's looking like a girl. When Sadie confronted Ed and she could see Harold;s new haircut, Ed said he " thought someone had cut Harold's hair and threw the curls in the fireplace". They were two and four at that time

Harold enjoyed living in Alaska when he was twelve years old; he learned to ice skate very well and played baseball under the midnight sun with the Anchorage Little League.

Harold married Donna Potter from Cove City during his first year of college at Wesleyan College in Rocky Mount NC. He transferred from Wesleyan and she transferred from UNC Chapel Hill to UNC Wilmington. Both studied Marine Biology.

Harold graduated from UNC Wilmington, worked for a record sales company in , then he got a job at Cherry Point MCAS until he could get a job in his education field with the NC State Marine Conservancy; he has been completely devoted his work for estuary protection in NC for over twenty five years. During this time he has invented several new instruments and processes to improve river bottom testing and improvement of marine life habitat. His efforts have been recognized by the State of North Carolina in the past.

In his off duty time he has traveled to Australia, Hawaii and several Atlantic and Pacific Islands in pursuit of the best wave (surfing). He was the second person in NC to receive an underwater diving certificate from the US Navy. With that training he dived the Florida underwater caves for many years and also used the training in his job of checking commercial flow of waste contamination in the estuaries of North Carolina.

During his married life with Donna both were deep sea divers and underwater photographers. Harold photographed sea animal and plant life and Donna did the writing of feature stories to match the photographs. Their work was featured in US Diver, NC State Wildlife and several other magazines. Harold won several photography awards for his photos of rare sea life.

After he and Donna divorced, he married Karen Edmonds and they had a son, Aaron Tyler Quidley, born 1 Sep 1990. Harold took Aaron para sailing when Aaron was four years old. Harold, Karen and Aaron were vacationing in Hawaii. He, Karen and Aaron also vacationed in the Bahamas and other exotic places.

Aaron is now a senior at North Carolina State University. When he graduates he plans to design and produce computer games for children. He has been playing the most complicated ones since he was about five. His grandfather remembers playing Mario with him and hopes they can play again in the future on a game he designs and produces.

In his later years Harold has become an avid Kayaker and Canoe person. He loves the outdoors and all of nature. No more fast life and very little danger, with complete silence, is his mode.

3 Sep 1955

Rovenia Simpson Rollison Quidley died (born May 18 1864). She was married to LHK David Farrow Quidley. When they married she was 17 and he was 32. They had eight children: Three were LHKs; they lived to be old men. Lighthouse

Keeper sons were Thomas Daniels Quidley, David Edward Quidley and Guy Chesterield Quidley. Three children of Rovenia and David died of tuberculosis in the 1920s and 1930s when a horrific TB epidemic killed hundreds on Hatteras Island.

In 1902 she became a widow with children ranging from two to twenty years old. The older two were already in the US Lighthouse Service and were able to give their mother and siblings some financial help.

As a child Rovenia was inclined to be a practical nurse and midwife; During her marriage she studied and learned the medical trade; after her husband died she practiced even harder; her transportation to make house calls was by horse and cart.. She was called the "Banker's Nurse" in reputation, human love and Christian deeds. In the National Geographic story in Dec 1933 she wanted to be called "Miss Bashi" to cover her identity. She delivered more than 1500 babies during her life; she treated wounds and healed sickness of any nature. She knew when the patient needed to go to Elizabeth City NC or Norfolk VA hospitals. She even made transportation arrangements and helped with the cost in a few cases.

After the US Navy sent a medical corpsman to serve the US Navy Weather Group at Buxton she worked, with him in all medical activities. They kept the islanders healthy and alive. He and she even made "life boat calls" to help injured or sick people on ships at sea.

The US Coast Guard provided the sea transportation.

Before the Navy sent the first medical technician to Buxton, Miss Roviene had to surgically remove a leg from a local fisherman who would have died had she not been there. Her entire adult life was spent helping and caring for her neighbors. From donations of thankful patients she made a good living for her family and then herself until she was 91. Her children graduated from high school or got their education while in military service. Each of her son's dreams was to get off the barren island of Hatteras and work to make a living.

28 Aug 1957

Dallas Jr presently as a civilian began School at University of North Carolina at Chapel Hill NC

1Sep 1957

Assigned USAFR 7th Dist OSI Durham Unit Reserve Duty

31 Oct 1961

Robert Pittman died of Cancer Age 60 (Born 11 Aug 1901)

1 Jan 1962

T Sgt Quidley with the USAF Recruiting Service as Public Relations Officer for NC, SC and parts of Georgia, began a series of TV Shows showing the uniforms and equipment used in the Air Force.

He used local students for models in his show. TV stations in Raleigh, Durham, Fayetteville, Greenville, Wilmington and Florence SC participated in the program sponsored by the Air Force Recruiting Service.

16 Jan 1962

To attend a public relations event in Winston Salem NC TSgt Quidley needed a fairly new and impressive appearing vehicle for a good impression and no trouble on the road. The new 1961 Nash Rambler four-door suited Dallas and the Transportation Supervisor, TSgt Bobby Barton. Bobby had the car washed and polished to perfection. When Dallas got in and started it there were no problems therefore the road from Raleigh to Winston Salem would be "a piece of cake" and if necessary he could speed a little. The trip up there was great

Dallas spoke at the event and then enjoyed socializing for a couple of hours. He then headed back to Raleigh by way of High Point NC. Due to the long meeting and a half day trip, he had to speed about sixty two miles per hour most of the trip back to Raleigh.

Just before getting to the city of Thomasville NC he came upon a two tiered overpass. About a mile from the overpass the traffic volume had changed, and Dallas slowed to fifty five miles per hour. Slowing down was the reason he is alive to write this story.

During the one hour trip from Winston Salem to the high rise overpass, Dallas had heard several times a metallic bang under the car. He had blamed the sound on what he thought was a rock being picked up from the highway and it banged on the drive shaft or something else. With no mechanical ability whatsoever he thought the sound would eventually go away when he got over a highway rock spill.

The bridge above the second tier of the road seemed to be the start of a crazy ride. Fear struck Dallas when the rear end of the car raised two feet, the drive shaft caught in a crack and that caused the car to head for the left rail. The drive shaft caught again and the car headed for the right rail, The car never touched either side of the concrete rail but repeated the course of crossing the road each time the drive shaft would catch. It repeated the process six times until the car came to a halt at the end of the long overpass bridge rail. It was if it was just parking itself on the right side of the road after the end of the overpass bridge. Each time the car had faced the rail Sgt Quidley could see the highway sections below with big trucks and cars swishing under him. He did not at that time know what was happening, but he thought his time to depart the earth had come.

No one can explain why the Air Force car was the only one on that section of the overpass. Later when people rushed to the car to see if the driver was still alive, it was determined that all of the other drivers had stopped their vehicles to watch the show. Several older drivers told Dallas that they had said some quick prayers for the car and driver of the blue USAF Nash Rambler.

Dallas was worn out from battling with the steering wheel which really was worthless during the ordeal. The bolts had come out of the drive shaft coupling one by one, making the banging noise. When all the bolts were gone the shaft dropped off at its front end of the shaft causing the car to go wild and scare its driver, and entertain everyone in sight. The Air Force sent another car and Dallas got home in time to have dinner with his wife and kids. He had a tale to tell, whether they believed him or not.

The many accident reports and paperwork that followed the accident might have caused the Air Force not to buy anymore Ramblers.

10 Dec 1963

TSgt Dallas Quidley received Orders for reassignment to Elmendorf AFB, Anchorage Alaska.

14 Dec 1963

Dallas, Sadie and the sons were given a Going Away Party at New Bern NC before the trip to Anchorage Alaska

19 Dec 1963

The Quidleys departed Raleigh for Alaska (in New 1963 Ford) via Seattle Washington.

1 Jan 1964

Dallas and family flew 707 jet to Anchorage AK from Seattle WA. Ed and Harold had fun on trip.

17 Mar 1964

Great Alaska Earthquake. After the big quake there were 10,000 light tremors in two weeks

Sgt Dallas Quidley, Sadie and two sons were living in Spenard, a Section of Anchorage Alaska, when The Great Alaska Earthquake hit. It lasted only a few minutes but it devastated Anchorage and other towns and villages within 60 miles of the epicenter. Sadie and the two boys, 10 & 12, were in the rented home. The house had a full basement; the only big damage to the house was it slipped on the under pining which were the outer walls of the basement. Sadie and the boys were able to get outside quickly and hold on to a picket fence in the front yard. She was fearful that the house would collapse or a gas line break would cause a fire or explosion. She remembers the noises coming from the entire Anchorage area. Glass breaking and the ground noises together were a bad chorus that made extra fear of their house sliding down the hill, or dropping into a very large sink hole beneath the house. Harold, the younger son ran out of the trembling house in his bare feet; due to the freezing condition and with a new snow on the ground, Sadie had to run back into the house when she realized he was in sock feet. Within three blocks of the house Sadie and Dallas found later that nearby several rows of homes in a subdivision on Cooke Inlet had wiggled and jiggled down the hill towards the Inlet. The sliding house scene was shown on the cover of Life Magazine the week of the quake. A color picture of a tilted house with a car still hanging in the carport was the cover picture; the home was Harold's school teacher's house. Our house was repairable, but Mr Smith's house was eventually bulldozed into bits and pieces.

Dallas was on duty that day at Elmendorf Air Force Base. His office was badly damaged but he got out of the building ok. He had to pull a few injured people out with him. They all got on a concrete sidewalk and laid down because the ground was throwing them around. The building and the entire yard dropped 8 feet.

The earthquake had created a sink hole beneath the entire yard. Later when viewing the building and yard looked as if the building was constructed in a large dried up swimming pool. The next lot (AF Base Headquarters building) did not have a sink hole under it. The view from the side walk allowed the viewers during the shaking to see the HQ parking lot from its surface view. At that eye level the view looking across the parking lot appeared that the asphalt was rippling like the waves on a river bed Also in view from the hole or sink was the flagpole on the HQ lot bending and whipping like a fishing rod with the flag touching the ground many times as the terrified people watched in fear and awe. When the trembling of the earth stopped, everyone had to get out of the yard by climbing a ladder to the level of the next door parking lot.

In looking at the building later it appeared that the building just gently and evenly went downwards. That same kind of sinkhole situation was the same in many places in the quake area during the earthquake.

Dallas was very concerned about his family because all phone lines were down, therefore getting home as quickly as possible was important to him. Finding his automobile not damaged, he began a rough four mile trip. The cracks in the roads caused him to have to turn around many times and find another path leading home; the damaged roads resulted in a four mile, six minute trip, becoming a three hour trip. When he finally reached home and he saw Sadie and the boys had not been hurt and were back into the house, they gave a thankful praise to The Lord.

In the ten days after the big quake, there were over 10,000 tremors which kept the population on edge and ready to run. It was a confusing period of time for many months after the disaster. Many people were homeless, many buildings were gone or badly damaged, the roads had to be completely redone, schools were knocked out and students reshuffled. Even the airplane runways were out of use for many months.

Sadie and Dallas were fortunate; in a few months after the quake they sold the new house they had recently built in Anchorage and moved further North in Alaska. TSgt Quidley had requested and got a transfer to Fairbanks Alaska, near North Pole City. The boys were excited about the trip. The family traveled all day across the mountains on 14 Dec arriving at Eilson AFB at night. The main incident of the trip was when a Badger ran along with the car trying to bite the wheels. Another thing that gave Dallas and Sadie a chance to say "Thank You God" was when Dallas turned off the engine of the car, the engine instantly froze. The car was towed away and it took several days in a garage to thaw. We found out later that on that day in late afternoon the temperature dropped as low as minus seventy degrees. During the winter months in both Anchorage and Fairbanks the car engine heater had to be plugged into an electric outlet at its parking space. The family acclimated to the severe cold in Fairbanks as they had done in Anchorage.

1 Aug 1966

The Quidleys began their drive down the ALCAN (Alaska-Canada) Highway, through Canada, to North Carolina.. Next assignment was to be at Stewart AFB NY where Dallas and Sadie had spent some time in 1951. They were on vacation in Oriental and New Bern NC for twenty days before going on to NY.

4 Aug 1966

Dallas Visited Maurice and Mioka Smestad in Hatton North Dakota. Dallas had not seen them in fourteen years.

5 Aug 1966

The family visited Marvin and Vickie Ulrich in Burnsville Minnesota. Dallas had not seen Marvin in fourteen years.

8 Aug 1966

Arrived in New Bern NC from Alaska

1 Sep 1966

Arrived at 2nd assignment to Newburgh NY

27 Dec 1967

Assigned USAF Recruiting Service Falls Church VA

20 Aug 1967

Moved to 3505 Fayette Ct, Dale City, Woodbridge VA

8 Jan 1968

Granna Will (Isaac Willoughby Swindell) died (Born 19 Feb 1879)

27 Apr 1968

Charles Childress died (born 14 Aug 1939) in Richmond VA. Charles was Lorena Quidley's husband. He was the Puegot Regional Auto Sales Manager

9 Feb 1969

Virginia Real Estate Sales License earned by Dallas E Quidley Jr.

31 Jul 1969

Mr Dallas Quidley Jr was retired from the USAF & departed for New Bern NC. Sadie and Dallas' new address was at 4709 Edgewood Dr. Whit Morgan was the RE Agent. Although Dallas had a job lined up, he was prepared to show his new resume.

8 Aug 1969

Dallas, a new civilian, began work for Sweetheart Cup Co (a subsidiary of the Maryland Companies.) On this date Mr Quidley met his new business partner Jack Webb in Fayetteville NC. Jack and Dallas became great partners and a super sales team. Jack and Dallas were expert salesmen and both had full knowledge of over five thousand items to sell which brought great earnings for ten years. One day Jack thought he had found a new career more lucrative. His interest in antiques and picture framing was wonderful for about a year. Then a short-time national recession put him into bankruptcy. He never fully recovered and he died "on his way back up". Jack was a wonderful business partner;

Jack taught Dallas what he knew as quickly as possible.. Dallas was fortunate to be found by Sweetheart Cup Co and be placed with a great salesman and a Christian. Jack was a real salesman and a great showman. He was tender hearted and kind, tall and a big person. Dallas was a thin, almost short and fairly quiet member of the team. Both members of the team loved to help customers with their sales to their customers. Dallas and Jack enjoyed giving samples of Sweetheart products to prospects. They saw that the use of disposable products benefited the customer by increased profits. Their sales efforts were jointly recorded and shared. They received large commissions during the ten years of their teamwork. They were the envy of their peers at work and sometimes their friends and neighbors at home.

Jack enjoyed his relatively short life. He had four children who received his zest to work.

2 Sep 1969

In the beginning Dallas' immediate Supervisor was Graham Gregory who recommended in July 1969 that the Regional Manager, Roy Stroud, hire Dallas when he retired from the Air Force. On this date Dallas flew to Owings Mills Md and was briefed about the Maryland Companies and positions of the corporate management team. He also attended a social session with all other newcomers (Sales Reps) from around the country.

15 Oct 1969

Wreck with Jack Quidley in Raleigh 18 Wheeler rear ended his Pickup Truck.

23 May 1970

Ed graduated from New Bern High School

5 Jul 1970

Bought Cottage on Beach St at Wrightsville Beach NC for Ed to live in while attending University of NC at Wilmington

3 Sep 1970

Dallas contracted with the US Postal Service to build a Post Office Building on the lot in Oriental NC. Dallas and his brother Jack were partners in the Post Office contract with the US Government.

2 Dec 1970

Dallas E Quidley Jr had breakfast and long conversation with his Grandfather Capt Tom Quidley at his home in Pamlico NC. Dallas made a tape of the conversation and also transcribed the conversation to a story of his grandfather's life.

7 Sep 1971

Formed Cape Hatteras Real Estate and Development Corp

20 Jan 1972

Ed married Brenda Ann Bender

15 Mar 1972

NC Real Estate Salesman License was converted from VA Real Estate license.

16 May 1972

Ed joined the USAF

22 May 1972

Harold graduated from New Bern HS

Jul 1972

Jason Edward Quidley was born Durham NC

4 Sep 1972

Gran (Cora Edwards Banks) died

7 Oct 1972

Brenda flew to San Antonio TX with baby Jason

14 Jan 1973

Dallas & Sadie drove to San Antonio TX to see Ed, Brenda and Jason.

24 Apr 1973

Ed transferred from San Antonio TX to Sunnyvale CA. He was trained in cryptographic electronics, digital machines and accessories. He then worked on electronic and computerized parts at the USAF facility in the Silicon Valley region. He became a specialist in building and repair of cryptographic instruments. His entire four years in the USAF, except for basic military training, was spent in Sunnyvale.

The Air Force work prompted him to get into the nuclear power field for later employment. It was also his basis for reentry into college to become a nuclear power professional..

1 Dec 1973

Dallas flew to Boston for a Sweetheart Cup meeting. This was his first knowledge of plastic straw and dinnerware manufacturing.

27 Dec 1973

Harold married Donna Potter.

4 May 1972

The Board of Directors and the Faculty of Onyang Academy, a former subsidiary of the University of South Korea, conferred upon Dallas Edward Quidley Jr the honorary degree of Doctorate of Humanities for his dedicated assistance to the people of Korea during their struggle to save their country from communist aggression. The Academy also recognized the fact that Dallas had already earned the requirement for this and another education degree, but due to travel and distance, those credits were never combined.

This honor was bestowed upon Dallas E Quidley Jr at a Dinner Meeting Of the Cape Hatteras Corporation. Colonel Arthur E K Brenner, former President of Onyang Academy presented the doctorate certificate and his congratulations. The dinner was held at the Holiday Inn of Nags Head NC. In attendance were William Hehl, Barbara Hehl, Sadie P Quidley, Dallas Quidley Jr, Col and Mrs Brenner and Miss Kathy Kelso.

20 Jul 1974

Thomas Pittman married Nancy Williams

15 Jul 1971

Dallas found Yuri Nosenko. Yuri was a Capt in the Russian Navy (USSR) Stationed at the Russian Embassy in Washington DC. He proved that he liked America very much. He also had fallen in love with a musical entertainer at the Capitol Club where many diplomats and politicians hang out.

MSgt Dallas Quidley was stationed in the Washington DC area at that time with the USAF Recruiting Service. Dallas read Reader's Digest religiously especially this type of story.

The Reader's Digest magazine had several stories on the case, and a third one on Gary Powers, a U2 pilot that had been shot down, captured and imprisoned in Russia. After Gary Powers of California was released from a Russian prison he informed the USA (CIA) that he could prove that Yuri Nosenko was a real defector and not a Russian Agent, nor was he a double agent. He swore that he had learned in the Russian prison that Yuri was in danger of Russian retaliation. Defector Nosenko was released from prison and was trusted again by the CIA.

Communist sympathizing news personnel made up stories to tear down this defector because they knew he had a story to tell that would help stop the Cold War. Gary Powers was Yuri's saving grace to be able to live in NC and have freedom from further involvement with the government. Dallas Quidley was very proud to hear of this decision. It was a great pleasure to Dallas to read of the reward of freedom and US citizenship for Yuri. Dallas then decided that he would try to find Yuri because he wanted to personally meet and thank him.

It was a blessing from God for Dallas to eventually come face to face with him. When Dallas met Yuri he swore to himself that he would not tell anyone about finding and knowing Yuri as long as Yuri lived. Dallas says that since Yuri was exploited by some news media and movie makers, he should at least tell the real story.

Yuri, after all the men and women who gave their lives for the USA, should become a World and USA Hero. By defecting from Russia his information surely slowed down the cold war. The communist in our own government did not like him or appreciate his defection

Dallas will only say that he had a friendship that he could trust, and vice versa for Yuri. The friendship lasted over thirty years and the last conversation was as exciting to Dallas as the first. Yuri was strong physically and in character; he was happy and contented to be an American. He had learned to speak English very well, dressed and acted as if he had been in the USA all his life. He loved to fish and hunt and had made many friends in America.

Dallas gained the trust of Yuri and his family. Yuri and every member of his family did not know that Dallas Quidley knew who Yuri was, or from where he came. Dallas found him by accident, recognized him immediately and called him by his assumed name. There was never a slip of the tongue.

He had to leave his own country because of communism. Every Good American should remember Yuri Nosenko because of what he did for them. He had a great life and died at 85. Dallas will certainly never forget him and he visits Yuri's grave as often as possible. A full tribute will someday come in Yuri's American name; wait for it.

23 Jul 1975

Dallas flew to San Francisco CA to see Ed, Bren & Jason

1 Aug 1976

Ed & Brenda moved to Wilmington NC He and Brenda bought a house in King's Grant subdivision.

1 Sep 1976

Ed returned to UNCW after serving four years in the Air Force

19 Dec 1976

Harold graduated from University of North Carolina (UNCW)

Feb 1977

Oakley M Parker Died (born 17 May 1892)

1 May 1977

Dallas & Sadie moved to Oriental from New Bern NC

16 Sep 1977

Sadie's sister Dot was visiting Sadie at the Sadie's new home in Oriental NC. They decided to drive to New Bern, 26 miles away, to do a little shopping. for some furniture. A new mattress was on Sadie's mind so she went to the mattress department and

Dot went to Home Decorations. Dot and Sadie were a little bit dainty and had forgotten their early childhood in the woods of Lukens NC. By this time they no longer walked flat footed but sort of glided across the floor smoothly like city folks. They didn't talk loud or scream with fear or great joy. They were ladies.

Sadie starts her furniture vigil at the bed, bed covers and mattress section. Several other real ladies, like themselves, and a young Marine are looking for the just right mattress. Sadie is really observing a bed with a beautiful bed cover and wonders if that is the exact one just for her. She lifts up the bed cover skirt and is set back by something that moved quickly under the bed. Her imagination ran wild. What was it?

The startling effect was soon gone and she was too curious not to look more closely. She pulled the bed skirt high enough to see completely under the bed, and she saw a 24 inch long black snake (Sadie remembers it as s about three or four feet). She knew if Dot or the female saleslady heard the word "snake!!" there would be catastrophic chase for the front door and many jugs and other glass ware would be broken, anything could happen.

Her decision was to go to the store office and report the snake. The manager said "Lady, we do not have snakes in the store, we are not a pet store. Thank you for telling me." To be kind to a foolish woman he followed her to the bed and lifted the bedcover; he saw the snake and then he ran back to the office, got a stick and came backed and killed the snake. The saleslady realized what the manager was doing. Also, she must have heard the word "Snake".

The saleslady jumped up on the bed she was showing to the Marine, and she began jumping up and down as if on a trampoline. She was screaming to the top of her voice "get on the bed" to all the other customers.

Sadie has never forgotten the day she found the snake in the furniture store.

10 MAY 1978

Dallas sold the US Post Office Building in Oriental NC to Jenkins Gas Co. In lieu of money payment for the building he decided to exchange his equity in the building for a thirty two foot Chris-Craft twin screw motor yacht. Jack received his equity in cash. Dallas named the new boat SWEETHEART.

Dallas and his brother Jack had built the building and leased it to the USPS. Economic times had changed with Jimmy Carter's presidency creating a lease agreement not worth the cost of doing business with the government. Since Dallas was the factory representative for Sweetheart Cup Company (The Maryland Companies Group of Owings Mills Md), the boat was used for many years to entertain business clients on fishing trips. The motor boat eventually was replaced by a 27 foot sail boat named ILLUSION. This boat was really more pleasure and cost much less to operate. It was also used more often. The ample and lusty winds of Oriental and Wrightsville Beach, plus having the beautiful ILLUSION, made sailing a wonderful hobby and pastime for a weary soul. The boating-urge waned as heart trouble came on the horizon.

18 Aug 1980

Capt Thomas Daniels Quidley died. (Born 15 Jul 1882) He was buried in the Pamlico Methodist Church Cemetery. He was the son of LHK David F Quidley and Rovenia Whedbee Rollison. He was born in Buxton NC. Because his father was ailing and unable to work when Tom was 16; he was hired out of the Keeper's Special Fund to temporarily fill vacancies at Cape Hatteras Lighthouse in Buxton NC He was paid by and was directly under the Senior LHK James Wilson Gillikin who was a friend of Tom's mother and dad.

Capt Tom had recalled to Dallas Jr his job, how he had to carry fuel in five gallon cans up the stairwell of the lighthouse to the rotunda, the glassed round room (housing for the powerful lamp and lens). The trip up the stairwell was a twice daily chore. Other tasks included lighting and extinguishing the lamp at the exact time. Once after completing the operation, it must have been in the morning, he dropped an empty five gallon fuel can and it hit every step to the bottom. He was glad he was the only one in the lighthouse to hear the awful bang as it rolled and hit every step to the bottom of the stairwell. When his summer employment ended and no other jobs were available, young Tom and his friend, Bateman Williams, caught the freight boat to Elizabeth City and the train from there to Norfolk VA. After a few days in Norfolk they got a job loading lumber on a large sailboat sailing to New York City.

The year Pop was 98, and having breakfast with Dallas Jr, then 65, he was able was able to explain the trip on the sailboat to New York in vivid details.

It was a four day trip up the Atlantic Coast to New York. He explained that half of the trip to New York was spent enduring a ferocious wind storm. The heavy seas had washed many pieces of lumber into the ocean. He even remembered which way the wind was blowing when they left Norfolk, and the changes of direction along the way.

At age 17, for three months, he was a deck hand on The Ventor which was owned by the Shelton Brothers. It took freight from Hatteras NC to Elizabeth City, NC. This was the same boat that transported Tom and Bate from Hatteras on their trip to Norfolk. This boat was a Chincoteaque-Bug-Eye design.

While he was 21 he served as a substitute Lighthouse Keeper at Bodie Island Lighthouse. With binoculars he witnessed the first flight of the Wright Brothers historic airplane on 3 Dec 1903. After Bodie Island he became a deck hand on the US Lighthouse Service buoy Tenders (boats), The Violet and The Bolt, during 1903 and 1904. Then on 13 Apr 1905 he became Keeper of the Neuse River Entrance Lighthouse when LHK John Ship became ill and retired.

During the September 1913 Hurricane the roof of the lighthouse was blown off.

During Jan 1918 the Neuse River froze with ice thick enough for a heavy man to walk safely over it. Even a few automobiles crossed further up the river during the "Big Freeze of 1918". Capt Quidley at the time was on leave at home in Pamlico Village with his wife and family.

Asst LHK James Samuel Miller was on duty during the freeze. Three weeks on duty with three weeks off was their schedule. Capt Tom had to pull a small boat five miles over the ice from Pamlico Village to the lighthouse to rescue LHK Miller. In Mar 1918 while on duty and alone LHK Miller suffered a stroke. He was able to signal a passing boat to come to his aid; The NC State Boat with Capt Will Dixon in charge took him to Pamlico Village.

Capt Tom Quidley was LHK at the Neuse River Lighthouse for thirty years. He was involved in many sea and river emergencies and had to perform constant rescues. On one he had to put his lighthouse boat into the water and rush to a tug boat on fire in the Neuse River; he rescued the Capt and crew but had to leave the burning boat which floated to a shallow beach where it burned to the water line. Dallas Jr remembers as a young boy the tug boat's engines were all that remained and were protruding above water. The wreck could still be seen by passing boats.

There were other boat fires, boat accidents (collisions), sinkings, storm related drownings and other emergencies. These events kept life-saving personnel busy and often in grave danger.

From 1907 through 1924 Capt Quidley and his wife, Lorena Rawls Quidley, were busy raising their own children along with two cousins of TDQ who came from Buxton NC to Pamlico NC to live with the Quidley family. The two cousins had come from one parent families living on Hatteras Island. Capt Tom went to Buxton by boat to get Nettie Farrow. John D Brady came on his own in a small sail boat when he was 16. Capt Tom was on duty and watched John's small boat come over the horizon of Pamlico Sound moving slowly and getting closer to the lighthouse at the entrance to the Neuse River. Cousin Tom was surprised that John could make that long trip, John was thankful to be welcomed by Tom and his family. Lorena, Tom and their children accepted both cousins as family; they lived happily in the Quidley household until they were grown and married.

Capt Tom helped John D Brady Sr get a job with the Lighthouse Department in Portsmouth VA where he served until he joined the US Army.; In France during WWI John was injured in battle by gas poisoning; he eventually became completely disabled and had to be permanently hospitalized; he and his wife, Susan Muse, had six children before John's battlefield injuries became apparent. He was in the Veteran's Home in Gulfport MS for the remainder of his life. Susan and Cousin Tom visited him many times thru the years.

John and Susan's children all did well in life. The boys were hard working men who made good livings for their families and were citizens of high respect. Paul Caraway Brady graduated from NC State University after serving four years in the US Navy during the Korean War. Paul's wife and family stood by him thru his education to be an Aeronautical Engineer. Paul was probably the only Aeronautical Engineer ever to come from Pamlico County NC. He worked at Cherry Point MCAS as an Aeronautical Engineer and retired from there He married Dora Simpson from Silver Hill and they have three children. Paul and Dora live in a beautiful home on Lower Broad Creek enjoying the life he always dreamed about.

Another son of John and Susan also earned a good education and did well. John D Brady Jr used his college education to become a head librarian in the main library in New York City. He retired and came back to Pamlico County and he bought the Dr St Elmo McCotter home in Bayboro. John D Jr was proprietor of a Bed and Breakfast establishment in the home for several years. He sold his home and business and is now in complete retirement enjoying the fruits of a long working life in New York City.

John D Brady Sr was fortunate to have a very intelligent and loving wife, who alone raised the family very well in John's absence.

Nettie married a local young man, John Tilman Paul, from Pamlico Village. Tillie was fortunate to get a job on the Diamond Shoals Lightship as a cook where he retired after 25 years of service; Tillie and Nettie's children all enjoyed long and happy lives. Roderick E Paul, the youngest and last survivor of Nettie's children died 14 Apr 2009 Rod was a special person in the village of Pamlico; he was always available to help anyone and was the most considerate human to every person in need that he ever met. Rod's memorial service was conducted by Rev Betty Jo Gwaltney Rogers and Rev Roy Rogers.(Man and wife ministers of the United Methodist Church). The Rogers were lifetime friends of Roderick and Mary Paul, his wife. The Church over flowed with people who remembered Rod's good life.

After the completion of the US Inland Waterway (Bay River to Pamlico River), the USLHS opened a new Life Saving Station and Buoy Maintenance Yard on the Inland Waterway canal at Hobucken NC. TDQ became the first Station Commander. He was responsible for all navigational equipment erected or anchored on the Pamlico and Neuse Rivers and in the Western Pamlico Sound. The Neuse River Lighthouse was closed and the building was removed from the piling. TDQ moved his family to their new home at the station at Hobucken in1934. Buel C Potter and Sultan R Carawan were his assistants

On 6 Jan 1936 Capt Tom lost his beloved wife Lorena to cancer. She was only 47 and had suffered with cancer for over ten years.

In 1939 the US Lighthouse Service became a part of the US Coast Guard.

On 30 Jan 1940 LHK Thomas Daniels Quidley retired from the US Coast Guard as a Civil Service Employee. He moved back to his home in the village of Pamlico. His brothers Bill, Dave and Guy had already retired from the USLHS and/ or the USCG. His brothers in Law, Duffy, Ellis, Guy, Wilson and Archie had also retired from the USLHS Service or the US Coast Guard. His sons Oscar and Dallas retired from the same. His son Thomas Gibbs Quidley served in the USCG at Hobucken USCG Station in WW 2. S1C Thomas Gibbs Quidley, on duty at the Hobucken Station in 1941 when Lt John F Kennedy stopped at the USCG Station with influenza.. Long before JFK was President Thomas G Quidley told family and friends about his assistance to the young Naval Officer who was very sick.

Capt Tom Sr was always proud to tell the story of his ancestors coming to America from Devonshire England as sailors working for the Crown transporting goods to and from various Colonial docks on the NC and Virginia coast, These facts by Capt Tom were proven by Colonial Records that are located in many NC County Courthouses. Capt William Quidley, TDQ's grandfather (five times removed) was shipwrecked at Buxton NC in 1747 while transporting goods for the Crown from Jamestown VA to ports in NC. Colonial records reveal that Capt William Quidley was paid four pounds for each trip and he received his last payment in 1747. Early Census Records in Dare, Currituck and Hyde Counties show that most all Quidley male ancestors were boat pilots or boat captains. There were three consecutive lighthouse keepers from LHK David Farrow through LHK Thomas Daniels Quidley to include LHK Dallas Edward Quidley Sr.

LHK Thomas Daniels Quidley was credited with the recruitment and retirement of at least fifty members , and his wife's family, into the US Life Saving Service, the U S Lighthouse Service and the US Coast Guard. He also helped at least half that number of neighbors and friends to find their careers in the military and the Maritime and Life Saving Service. TDQ's grandson, MSgt Dallas

Edward Quidley Jr beat his grandad's record with over 400 enlistments into the US Air Force for Nurses, regular Airmen and Pilot traininee candidates over a four year period. Sgt Quidley's recruited while on assigned duty with the USAF Recruiting Service. Capt Tom did his procurement in his off duty time and out of love for everyone, Dallas Jr did his recruiting as a part of his job and for love of his country.

8 Nov 1980

Bacco (The cat sent to Sadie from Dallas III while he was in California) died at the Vet's Office in Havelock NC of cancer.

1 Jun 1980

Dallas saw a young man hitch hiking on Hwy 17 just outside Surf City NC, The young man said he was going to Wilmington to seek a job and that he had recently graduated from Pender Co High School. He was going to spend the night at a friend's house north of Wilmington. He said a friend also had some prospects for a job. He was very personable and highly intelligent; he had been around because his dad had recently retired from the U S Navy. Dallas suggested that maybe he should join the Navy or even the US Air Force; he explained that he had difficulty blending with people of authority and they had imposed their will on him. Dallas never told him he might know his mother at the place of business Dallas called on in Wilmington.

The young man appeared secretive about his life. He had passed the test for Dallas to know this was a kid worth helping. Maybe he and his dad could not understand each other. Dallas thought what if my son had asked a stranger for needed advice, would he appreciate any help Ed or Harold could get? Dallas read friendship and thankfulness in Paul's eyes. He saw in Paul's young face a relief to find someone to talk with and that he had finally found mutual understanding. It helped Dallas to meet Paul because his own two boys had recently left the nest and he was concerned about their coping with being an adult in the big world.

When the rider got out of the car Dallas handed him his card and asked him to show it to his mother at Maola Ice Cream Co where she worked. He also told him to call him if he needed a reference for a job. Dallas immediately had in mind several places Paul might look for employment. Paul appeared to be honest and to have a heart of gold but suffering from very low self-esteem. It was obvious that he had the ambition to work, and had already learned many home construction jobs. His dad had given him a wonderful earlier life no matter what the problems were now.

In about a week Paul called him about the job he got the next day after getting the ride, and how much the advice Dallas gave him about life helped him on that job and in his thinking for the future. Right then Dallas decided to see what he could do for Paul Nawcum Williams III. Paul became Dallas' big project for as long as necessary.

In less than a year Paul showed Dallas that he was improving in courage, faith in God and in himself. Paul had been near self-destruction and needed a friend desperately when Dallas came along Hwy 17 and saw him thumbing. He needed someone to tell him that God loved him and so did they. He would come to see Dallas and Sadie, or Dallas would bump into him during business rounds in the city; he was always happy to see Dallas and each time he had a good report to present. When he came for a visit to the house Dallas and Sadie could see him coming across the golf course because he always took a good short cut; he was no dummy.

On two occasions Dallas asked Paul how he and his dad were doing. He said his dad did not show any interest in him and actually told him not to come back home. Dallas talked Paul into letting him go to his home and both of them talk with his dad. On those two occasions Dallas drove Paul to see his mom and dad, Paul would come out crying; He said he thought his dad had lost his mind. Dallas thought maybe Viet Nam naval service had caused his dad to be emotionally upset. or he had a deeper mental problem. Finally Dallas decided he would not interfere with the situation again, but would encourage Paul to work out his own problems in due time.

For more than a year Dallas and Sadie had helped Paul. One day he came to Dallas with everything he owned in a backpack, Paul thanked Dallas for all his help; he told Dallas he was going to Florida to live. He said he had learned the building trades and could get a job easily. He wanted to get away from the area and try a new environment. Dallas agreed with him that this would be a good move, gave him a few bucks and told him goodbye. They prayed together as they had often done in the past year. Tears flowed from Paul's eyes and also from Dallas.

Soon after arriving in Florida he found a girl that also needed a home and attention. They married and had two beautiful children. As soon as both of them reached maturity they realized that married life had only worsened their problems, they divorced. Both remarried. Paul married a young widow lady with four small children.

Over the next fifteen years Paul helped raise the children and was a good husband to his wife. All four children received either college degrees or high school diplomas. Evidently they had a good family life. The family had moved to the mountains of Colorado after the marriage.

Dallas lost contact with Paul soon after his second marriage and his move from Florida. With more than fifteen years of silence, Paul found Dallas and Sadie on the internet. Dallas is proud that Paul remembers his sacrifices in helping to get him over the teen age hump. He is proud that Paul is a Christian and a republican. His excited electronic message is copied from the e mail as follows:

TO: DALLAS QUIDLEY FROM PAUL N WILLIAMS Tuesday May 24, 2011 12:11 PM

Subject: Long Time

WOW! I have tried to locate you for years. Last contact was in1994 when you were starting a new Development in Oriental NC. That's when I told you I was crazy for someone I had just met. Well, I married her and we have been together since, fifteen years and counting. The oldest boy we have is Richard and he will be graduating from college June 15th. The youngest, Adrian, will be graduating from high school next week.

I will be 49 this year in July. It's been a long road for me but without your mentoring in my youth I would not have made it this far. I am very grateful for meeting you and want you to know you will always be in my heart. I have not forgotten you or the things you did for me. It takes an incredible person like yourself to help a down trodden and lost person such as I was. You inspired me to be a better person than I thought I could be, I thank you for being there for me when I needed human compassion and could feel none. If I had never met you, my life would have been a lot shorter. I was on the path to self-destruction until you showed me that all humans aren't bad. It also gave me hope for a future that I had not a clue was there. In the past 15 years I married Judy and have helped her raise her kids. I had to abandon my own because my ex hid them from me. I moved to the Rockies up toward Aspen Colorado working as a carpenter at $40 per hour until the bottom fell out here. I owned my own home of four bedrooms, bath and two car garage. My two cars and the home were repossessed. I now own a mobile home and have two used cars. I don't find work as often *as I use to do. If it were not for Judy working we would be hurting. I used to build houses and now I am glad to get chance to build a garage. You know I have always been a hustler when it came to finding work. I will always prevail because of the confidence you inspired in me. Much love to you. Please call or email me anytime. I miss you. With Love*

Paul

3 Jan 2009

Actor Martin Patterson Hingle, a distinguished actor, died in Wilmington NC, He was 84 years old. He was survived by his wife Julia of Carolina Beach NC. Other survivors were two sisters, five children and eleven grandchildren. He was born in Miami Florida on 19 Jul 1924. He came to Wilmington to play in "Maximum Overdrive ". Other movies he made included: Hang 'Em High, Norma Rae plus many more.

Dallas met with him on several occasions in his home and found him to be a very interesting and gentile person. Those qualities in anyone is appreciated and never forgotten.

21 Feb 1983

Lucien A Madore (Ret Col-USAF) died in Florida, born Dec 4, 1905

1 Mar 1984

Dallas and Sadie moved from Oriental to Echo Farms in Wilmington NC

1 Aug 1985

Dallas and Sadie sold their home in Echo Farms and moved moved to 933 Hood Dr Wilmington NC

26 Nov 1985

John Chumley died of cancer (born 12 Sep 1928). John was Dallas' roommate in the New Kaijo Barracks in Tokyo Japan in 1951 & 1952 John was a budding surrealist artist while in the US Air Force. He had graduated from Ringling School of Art in Florida prior to his arrival in Tokyo.

After military service John and his family lived on a farm in the Virginia hills. The farm was exactly like it was during the Civil War with a military hospital, a grist mill at a dam on a running water creek. There were also five farm houses. Sadie and Dallas visited John and his family one time while Dallas was stationed in Washington DC. John and

Dallas enjoyed their first and last reunion since Tokyo. John showed Dallas one his houses and said, "You and Sadie and the boys can come here and live if we have a bad national depression." Dallas remains thankful for John's enduring friendship and will remember those words forever.

His art became very famous. At one time every US Embassy in the World had one of his paintings hanging on the wall;. You can GOOGLE John Chumley Artist and view his work. If you get the right web site you will see Dallas' memorial to his friend.

1 Jun 1987

Gregory A Mathews came to work for Sweetheart Cup Co immediately after graduating from NC State University where he was a football star. His product training was conducted by Dallas on board First Priority sailboat. The first day of training was conducted during an all-day sail in the Atlantic Ocean off the coast of Wrightsville Beach NC. Greg enjoyed his first day of training. Dallas had never conducted an orientation and sales training course while sailing. Greg thought the sail-sales training was good for his future and made him a better employee of the Company.

Gregory A Mathews has never stopped learning the trade. He performed in a superior manner with Sweetheart Cup Co until it was bought. Greg found a better position with another paper Company. According to Dallas Quidley Greg Mathews is the best salesman he has ever seen.

Greg and Dallas had worked together eight years with Sweetheart Cup Co. They became a perfect team in paper sales, then partners in real estate development and real estate sales. Greg became more than a sales partner, he became an adopted son. Greg calls him Pop.

In Dallas and Sadie's ageing, Greg has been a consistent helper to Dallas and Sadie. His visits have been appreciated. Every Christmas season he arrives on the 27th Dec and leaves on the 29th December. They have met him, and returned him, to the airport the same date and time for the past fifteen years. He is their big Christmas present.

Greg shares his frequent flyers points with Dallas. Pops knows who to call when he needs to take a trip. Sadie has taught Greg much about gardening, trees and taking care of his home. Greg often calls her for advice. The Quidleys and Greg have a mutual admiration society for life.

Jul 1987

First Priority Real Estate & Management Services was incorporated.

10 Aug 1987

Dare Co Commissioners final approval for Hatteras Pines subdivision.

1 Sep 1987

First Priority Company moved to 3909 Oleander Dr Wilmington NC with four employees.

Dallas Edward Quidley Jr.

15 Sep 1987

ERA added. Dallas flew to Wichita KS for ERA School

2 Oct 1987

Real Estate office robbed during night and cash returned after the robber was caught by Wachovia Bank employees.

10 Nov 1987

Cape Hatteras Dev Corp sold Hatteras Pines to Buxton Group. Dallas Quidley Jr was President of CHDC. Arthur Brenner was Vice President and William Hehl was Secretary Treasurer. The Corporation had accomplished its goal to buy Dallas' ancestral land, and prepare it for sale. It was a brutal task due to the amount of government interference but the group was pleased that a break even point was reached.

22 Dec 1987

Arthur Brenner (Ret Col USAF) died in Chatham MA of Liver Cancer. (Born 16 Jun 1915)

5 Aug 1988

First Priority ERA moved to 2250 Shipyard Blvd with 22 Real Estate sales persons

7 AUG 1988

James Calhoun Reno died (born 10 Jan 1930 TN)
He was VP of Bowater Paper Co

13 APR 1989

Dallas notified that Wachovia had incorrectly
submitted two Quarterly Tax Reports with
wrong ID numbers. Trouble with NC IRS began
a nightmare that lasted two years.

1990

Aaron Tyler Quidley was born in Raleigh NC,
son of Harold & Karen Quidley. When Aaron
graduates from NCSU he plans have a Master's
Degree in Computer Engineering. He is planning
to write and make children's computer games.

23 JAN 1991

Grandma Eva (Eva Mae Banks Pittman died (born
18 Nov 1909)

14 FEB 1991

Grandady Dallas (LHK Dallas Edward Quidley Sr)
died (born 2 Dec 1908)

8 Mar 1991

Michael B Stonestreet resigned from Cape Hatteras Development Corporation.

31 Mar 1991

Closed Home Owners Association Management (HOAM)

21 May 1992

John K Gant died (born 9 Dec 1919) was a Korean War Hero and POW. His B29 Shot Down. He was prisoner for 4 years; then, went to USAF Recruiting in NC with Dallas QuidleyJr.

15 Apr 1993

Oscar D Quidley died (born 6 Dec 1912) married Martha Leary Muse on 28 Nov 1935.

1 Jan 1994

Dallas E Quidley Jr retired from Sweetheart Cup Co & Ft Howard Paper Co with over twenty five years of service. He was honored with a regional meeting dinner party in Charlotte NC. The Regional and District Managers gave him a diamond and ruby Corporation Ring and a letter of congratulations for his many years as the top salesman for several products. Dallas had been World Wide leader in ice cream cones sales many times. The Eat It All Cone Company which Dallas represented had plants in Europe and Indonesia plus seven plants in the USA. He was often called The Cone King.

JUL 1995

Tyler E Stonestreet was born to Denny Allen Stonestreet and Melissa Fipps. Denny was legally blind and he got custody of Tyler after divorcing Melissa. DEQ Jr and Sadie helped to raise Tyler until he was six. They are Tyler's Granma and Grandpa for life. Denny is like a Son since Dallas helped his ailing dad, Jerry raise him from the age of 13 to 30.

1 JAN 1995

Dallas Quidley applied for and got a temporary job in the Engineering School at NC State University in Raleigh. It was to be a four week position in the Director's Office of the Electrical and Computer Engineering Department; Dallas wanted to work in a job where he could learn how to operate a computer. The job lasted four years until Dallas "threw in the towel" for working. That was just before he had to have Quadruple Heart Bypass Surgery.

He had enjoyed the work at NCSU, but his most rewarding event in which he was directly responsible was when two young men arrived for an official visit from East Germany. The ECE Director told Dallas to entertain the two distinguished visitors. Dallas could show them whatever they wanted to see, on or off the campus, to keep them happy. After they had seen the Campus and Raleigh, they spent two days looking around coastal NC. They had never eaten in a cafeteria, so they were given the chance to eat at a Golden Coral Restaurant; they had never seen a movie being made so they visited two movie making sites in Wilmington while Big Fat Greek Wedding was in progress: They met some movie stars and they rode in a stretch limo around New Hanover County. Dallas' Friends in Wilmington made all those things possible.

The NCSU guests had never seen the ocean, therefore a trip to Wrightsville Beach was in order; Although the water was cold, they wanted to wade in the surf.

Jens Kober and Olaf Zimmerhackl from Dresden Germany will never forget America. They are now Production Engineers in Dresden Germany working for AMD Global Industries. They are happily married and have at least one child each. Dallas gets a family letter and Christmas card from both families every December.

25 Oct 1995

Willis Rabik died in CA (born 25 Aug 1929)

7 Feb 1997

Lena Mae Swindell Quidley died (born 22 Apr 1909)

1 Apr 1997

Dallas replaced Greg Matthews in Raleigh NC as Territory Manager. This was the second time living in Raleigh. This time Dallas and Sadie lived in the

North Hills area. They lived in a very busy area and never really got to know many neighbors. The first four year residency was in the Longview Gardens area. This was where Ed went to school in the first grade at Longview Elementary School. They had great neighbors including Graham Gregory and his family, and Olen and Mayfield Watson and their family.

16 Oct 1998

Virginia Q Brown died. (Born 25 Aug 1914) She married William Hugh Brown on 16 Nov 1936. They had one son William Hugh Brown Jr. He married Linda Hughes from Colerain NC. Hugh and Linda have two children and three grandchildren. Hugh Earned a Master's Degree in Audio Visual education. He is now retired and enjoys his grandchildren.

23 May 1999

Reid McLawhorn died (born 31 Feb 1923) Reid had retired from the chemical industry and then became a real estate salesman at First Priority Real Estate. He was a personal friend of Dallas and Sadie Quidley and he lived on the water in Wrightsville Beach NC. He died of cancer.

18 Jun 1999

Dallas Jr had Quadruple Cardiac Surgery Rex Hospital in Raleigh NC. He had waited five years after discovery of cardiac problems for the safe and right time. The Doctors and Dallas felt he was not in a life threatening mode yet, and the present blood pump being used had not been perfected. Advisors developing the pump said they were working on a new model. Dallas was willing to wait for the improved pump that would not pump too much blood to the brain. This day turned out to be the correct time and the right place to get four new arteries and a longer life.

Dallas and Sadie had driven from New Bern to Raleigh for a semi-annual catheterization. After the procedure was completed Dr Robert Brunner, his Cardiologist, told Dallas and Sadie that he was afraid to wait any longer that the quadruple heart operation should be done as soon as possible. Dallas had one functioning artery and that five were ether totally or near collapse. Angina had almost completed its course.

It was decided that the operation would be done the next morning at 7 a.m. A bed and room for the night was assigned at Rex Hospital but the operation would be performed by a Wake Hospital heart surgeon. The usual preparations and instructions began after Dallas got into his bed. The body shaving, the marking of the body for each incision and the final briefing by the anesthetist, the surgeon and the Nurse on duty for the evening were all done. Dallas listened carefully and followed all instructions to the letter except from the surgeon; His instructions: "A video of the operation is on the video player I am leaving. It will show you what I will be doing to you tomorrow. Please watch it before you go to sleep"

Dallas responded quickly, "Please take it with you and if you need to see it again, you watch it. I believe I will be too sleepy to watch." He also told the doctor that if he did not wake up after the operation, he thanked him for his efforts anyway. He also told Sadie that he did not worry about the operation because The Lord was with him always. Dallas Jr told Sadie not to tell anyone about the operation scheduled for the next morning at 7 am except his sons,

19 Jun 1999

From 6:45 a.m. to 10:30 a.m the surgery team did an outstanding job and Dallas woke up and thanked Dr John Zeock as he had promised.

10 JUL 1999

Ed married Susan Rogers.

11 SEP 2001

Terrorist attack twin towers. The World Changed Greatly.

16 OCT 2001

Charlie C (Whitey) Welborn died (born 3 Oct 1924) USMC Retired. WW2, (Korea and Viet Nam Hero)

5 JUL 2001

Denny and Tyler Stonestreet departed New Bern NC

21 SEP 2003

Thomas Gibbs Quidley Sr died Spartanburg SC (born 13 Aug 1920)

24 JUL 2004

Two brothers, a friend and an older lady were killed this date by a drinking driver. William Carlton Carawan Jr, brother of the other two brothers was the driver; he had borrowed a girlfriend's car and was drinking and trying to scare the younger boys. At one hundred miles per hour he came upon an overpass, broadsiding a car as it came out of an exit on his right. The older driver, a lady had planned to cross William's lane and proceed in the direction from which he came. She died and her husband was injured for life. An eighteen year old unnamed friend of Linwood Carawan died instantly along with the others.

The driver was hospitalized for several weeks and is now serving a fifteen year prison sentence. Although this story ended tragically, Dallas Quidley remembers when Linwood had been in another bad accident which left him completely paralyzed. Dallas met Linwood and his dad, William C Carawan Sr. in the dentist office. Linwood was like a baby and could not even talk. He made joyful noises for approval and frantic noises for disapproval. Dallas was wearing special wrist watch that took Linwood's eye With excitement and his usual motions, he asked Dallas to let him see and feel of the watch. The watch caused Dallas to begin a conversation with him. Dallas soon understood most of what Linwood was saying. He told Dallas about his accident, with his dad filling in the details. His dad explained that Linwood's mom had recently died of cancer and he had to take care of his youngest son.. Linwood liked the watch Dallas